"I don't want a [baby]"

"I imagine you don't. But you have one."

"This is ridiculous." He rose, but he didn't come around the desk. This whole scenario was a nightmare. And any minute he'd wake up. Please…

He took a deep breath, searching for control. Searching for sanity. Glancing down at his appointment list, he registered her name.

"You're Gemma Campbell?"

"That's right. Fiona's sister."

Her tone was almost uninterested, and for the first time he realized why. She was here to hand over a baby and leave, he thought with a jolt of sick dismay. "And…and Fiona told you this…this baby was mine."

"She did." For the first time he saw the glimmer of a smile behind the weariness. "Though I might have guessed. Have a look for yourself." And she lifted the blanket away from the baby's head.

It was all he could do not to gasp.

Dear Reader,

I do like handing my doctors' interesting cases, and I do like dreaming up fantastic consultations. So I thought, what if... ("what if" are my favorite author words) my gorgeous heroine—a woman Nate's never met in his life—arrived for a consultation, but instead of offering Nate something ordinary like an infected toe, she's handing him a baby. "Here you are, Doctor—here's your daughter!"

I had a heap of fun writing *To the Doctor: A Daughter*. I hope you have as much fun reading it.

I'd love your feedback—contact me through my Web site at www.marionlennox.com

Happy reading!

Marion Lennox

To the Doctor:
A Daughter

Marion Lennox

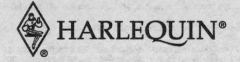

TORONTO • NEW YORK • LONDON
AMSTERDAM • PARIS • SYDNEY • HAMBURG
STOCKHOLM • ATHENS • TOKYO • MILAN • MADRID
PRAGUE • WARSAW • BUDAPEST • AUCKLAND

ISBN 0-373-06411-X

TO THE DOCTOR: A DAUGHTER

First North American Publication 2003

Visit us at www.eHarlequin.com

Printed in U.S.A.

CHAPTER ONE

'SHE's your baby.'

'I beg your pardon?' Maybe he hadn't heard right. It was the end of a long day and Dr Nate Ethan was thinking of the night to come. This woman was his last patient and then he was free.

Donna would be waiting. That was a good thought. Tonight was the Terama Jazzfest and he was never too tired for jazz.

Meanwhile, it looked as if he had to cope with a nutcase.

'Excuse me?' he said again, and forced himself to focus. Nutcase or not, she might be in trouble. He didn't know who she was and with unknown patients nothing should be assumed.

So concentrate…

She could well be a single mum, he decided, noting the absence of a wedding ring. After six years of country medicine he noticed such things almost without trying. She was in her late twenties, he guessed, though the strain on her face made her look older. Faded jeans, a T-shirt that was old and misshapen and the knot of frayed ribbon catching back her mass of black curls suggested financial hardship.

What else? She looked as if she was in trouble, he thought. Her dark eyes—brown, almost black—were made even darker by shadows of fatigue, and her finely boned face was etched with worry.

'How can I help you?' he asked, his tone gentling. Hell, they had it hard, these single mums. A little boy, maybe four years old, was clinging to a fistful of her T-shirt, and she carried a baby that looked no more than a few weeks old.

'I'm not here to ask for help.' Her tone was as weary as her face. She seemed like someone at the end of her tether. 'I'm here to hand over what's yours.' She lifted the baby toward him. 'This is Mia. She's four weeks old and she's yours.'

Silence. The silence went on and on, stretching into the evening. Outside a kookaburra started laughing in the clump of eucalypts hanging over the river and the laughter seemed crazily out of place.

Would he help?

Gemma was feeling sick. Everything—her entire future—hung on what happened in the next few minutes.

Was he as irresponsible as her sister?

He looked…nice, she decided. But, then, Fiona had looked 'nice' and where had that got her?

Maybe, like Fiona, he was too good-looking for his own good. He was seriously handsome, in a way that could make him a candidate for the next James Bond movie. Tall, with great bone structure and a deeply tanned complexion, his size didn't make him seem aloof. His burnt red hair was coiling forward over his brow in an endearing twist, and his deep green eyes sort of twinkled even when he wasn't smiling.

He had great bones, she decided—the sort of bones that made a girl want to…

Whoa. She wasn't going down that road. Never again. That was the sort of feeling that got her into this mess in the first place. The sort of feeling Fiona had had…

And on the other side of the desk…

She was a nutcase, Nate decided. Heck, as if he didn't have enough on his plate.

Donna was waiting.

'Um… I've never met you before,' he ventured, and she nodded.

'No.'

'Then how—'

'Hey, she's not *my* baby,' she told him, meeting his eyes and holding them with a look that was direct and strong. Challenging. 'She's yours.'

'I don't—'

'My sister is…' She caught herself at that and she bit her lip while the shadows under eyes seemed to darken. 'My sister *was* Fiona Campbell. She was a locum here until last December. Do you remember her?'

His eyes widened. Fiona Campbell. He certainly remembered Fiona, and he remembered her with a certain amount of horror. 'Yes, but—'

'You went to bed with her?'

To bed. His gut gave a stupid lurch. *You went to bed with her.* Fiona…

Dear God, this was the stuff of nightmares. 'Yes, but—'

'There you are, then,' she said wearily. 'One and one make three. Fiona had your baby a month ago and she died the day after delivery.'

This time the silence seemed to reach into eternity. The woman didn't say another word—just sat and watched, giving him time to take it in. The child by her side was silent as well. The little boy held onto her shirt fiercely, as if keeping in contact with her was the only important thing in his life. And the baby was sound asleep, nestled in a swathe of pink blankets and oblivious to the world around her.

Fiona Campbell.

Hell.

She'd been the flightiest locum. Graham, his uncle and

his partner in this tiny country medical practice, had been ill and Nate had been desperate. Fiona had been the only doctor who'd answered his advertisement.

So she'd bubbled into his life, sparkling with life and totally fascinating. She had been gorgeously, stunningly beautiful.

She had also been a little bit…mad?

It had taken him time to see it. She'd lived her life to the full, hardly sleeping, partying, accepting dates with anyone who'd asked her and running on sheer adrenalin.

And from the time she'd met him she'd wanted to sleep with him.

'We're made for each other,' she'd told him, seductive in her sheer audacity. 'You're the most gorgeous doctor I know. And what about me? Aren't I the most gorgeous doctor you know?'

She was at that, he'd conceded. He'd been between girl-friends, she'd been bewitching in her desire to take him to her bed…and, well, a man was only human.

As soon as he'd slept with her, though, he'd known it had been a mistake. A major mistake. There had been lay-ers beneath her surface he could scarcely imagine. She had been driven—and he didn't know why.

So he'd slept with her. Just the once. And that had been it. He'd had the sense to back away fast. And when Graham had recovered and Fiona had left, he'd felt nothing but relief.

But when he'd slept with her…

'We were careful,' he said, thinking it through and thinking fast. He was hardly speaking to the woman in front of him. He was speaking only to himself. He knew enough to avoid unsafe sex. 'She said she was protected—and I used a condom as well. Of course I did.'

'Of course you did, and bully for you.' The woman shrugged. 'But are you sure she didn't get to it first?'

His eyebrows hit his hairline. 'What on earth do you mean?'

'I mean what Fiona wanted Fiona generally got. And it seemed she wanted your baby.'

'That's ridiculous.'

'Is it?' She shrugged again and her shrug was a gesture of bone-weariness. 'Fiona told me this is your baby. She said she chose you as the father, and if she decided she wanted your baby then I wouldn't have put it past her to lie about protection—and even damage your condom before you used it. But if you'd like to do a DNA test…'

He was staring at the baby like he'd have stared at a coiled snake. She had red hair. Red hair! 'It's impossible.'

'She named you as the father, using a statutory declaration before the baby was born.' She gestured to her handbag. 'She even signed it in front of a Justice of the Peace. Do you want to see?'

'No!'

'Suit yourself.' She rose and proffered the bundle in her arms. 'But like it or not, this is your daughter, Dr Ethan. Her mother's dead so that makes her all yours.'

To say Nate was dumbfounded was an understatement. He sat in his chair as if rooted to the spot and his head couldn't take it in. He opened his mouth and what came out was feeble. 'I don't want a baby!'

'I imagine you don't. But you have one.'

'This is ridiculous.' He rose but he didn't come around the desk. It was as if he was afraid to come close. This whole scenario was a nightmare. A ridiculous nightmare. And any minute he'd wake up. Please…

'I told you…we were careful.'

'Fiona was never careful.'

He took a deep breath, searching for control. Searching for sanity. Glancing down at his appointment list, he registered her name.

'You're Gemma Campbell.'

'That's right. Fiona's sister.' Her tone was almost uninterested and for the first time he realised why. She was here to hand over a baby and leave, he thought with a jolt of sick dismay. She was here to hand over a baby that had nothing to do with her—and everything to do with him.

'And…and Fiona told you this…this baby was mine.'

'She did.' For the first time he saw the glimmer of a smile behind the weariness. 'Though I might have guessed. Have a look for yourself.' And she lifted the blanket away from the baby's head.

It was all he could do not to gasp.

He'd seen baby photos of himself. He'd been born with the burnt red hair he had now. It was unusual hair—dark, tinged with black and curling into a thick mane. He had dark skin and green eyes and eyebrows that were definitely black.

He'd been a gorgeous baby, his mother had told him, and this baby was certainly that. Gorgeous.

She lay in her cocoon of blankets, one fist curled into a tiny ball at the edge of her rosebud mouth. She had tight, tight curls, a deep burnt red in colour, and her tiny, finely etched eyebrows were as black as…

As black as his.

Dark skin and red hair and black eyebrows. Her colouring was really rare.

As was his.

She'd have his green eyes, Nate guessed, and as he stared down at her he felt something twist deep inside. It was a gut-wrenching twist that had him clutching the edge of his desk for support.

'You still want to tell me she's not yours?' Gemma's eyes rested on his, not without sympathy. But her voice was implacable.

'Yes... No.' The world seemed to spin. A daughter. He had a daughter. 'But—

'I told you, what Fiona wants...*wanted*, Fiona got. And it seems that she took one look at you and decided that she wanted your child.'

He stared at her blindly and then sat heavily back down behind his desk.

'Hell!'

'Yes,' Gemma said softly. She sat as well, waiting for him to come to terms with what she'd just said.

'Gemma, I'm thirsty.' It was the little boy, speaking for the first time. He was still clutching her T-shirt but he was staring at Nate as if he was afraid of him.

At least this was something concrete. Thirst. He could cope with thirst.

He couldn't cope with a baby.

He rose, filled a paper cup from the water cooler and handed it to the child. The little boy stared at it as if it might just contain poison, but then his thirst got the better of him and he drank.

It was a respite—albeit a minor one—but it gave Nate breathing space. Space to know one thing for certain.

'Whether I'm her father or not is immaterial,' he said flatly. 'I can't have her.'

'Whether you're her father or not isn't the least bit immaterial. She's yours.'

'I don't want her.'

'You'd rather she was adopted by strangers?'

That was another kick to the guts. His eyes flew to hers. 'What do you mean?'

'Just that. It's you or adoption. Take your pick.'

'But you... You're obviously caring for her.'

'Yes. But I can't keep her.'

'Why not?' His voice came out almost as a croak. He sounded sick. Well, why wouldn't he sound sick? He surely felt like that.

'I have my own life—' she started.

He wasn't buying into this. She'd taken on the baby's care already. What could be more logical than asking her to keep up the good work? 'This is your sister's child.' He forced his voice to stay steady, despite thoughts that weren't the least bit steady. His thoughts were close to panic. 'And you have a child already.' He took a deep breath, thinking it through.

'Look, crazy or not... If it's proven that she's mine— and I'm not conceding that yet, but if she is—then I guess I'm stuck with child support. I'll pay you to keep her.'

Her eyes flashed anger at that. 'Oh, that's very generous. I don't think.'

'Well, what else do you expect me to do?'

'Shoulder your responsibilities,' she snapped. 'And not offload them onto me. I've had enough.'

He focused on her then. Really focused.

She'd had enough.

It was true, he thought. Her face was pale with strain and her eyes were dark pools of exhaustion.

What had she said? That Fiona had died in childbirth. It sounded unbelievable. Vibrant, alive Fiona.

Crazy Fiona.

But Gemma had lost her sister.

'How did she die?' he asked, his tone softening, and he saw her eyes widen in surprise. She hadn't expected compassion.

'I don't...'

He took a deep breath. 'Look, maybe we'd better have the whole story. Did she die of eclampsia?'

'No.' She shook her head. 'She died of kidney failure caused by her pregnancy combined with uncontrolled diabetes. She died because she didn't give a toss for her life—or the lives of her children. Both of them.'

Both of them.

Both...

Wasn't the little boy hers, then?

Nate stared at the child, stunned, and then he looked at Gemma. There were similarities, he thought. Woman and boy were both dark-haired and pale-skinned. They looked like mother and son. But...maybe there were stronger similarities between the child and what he remembered of Fiona.

And the girl herself reminded him of Fiona. Though there were marked differences. Fiona had been almost ethereal in her beauty. She'd dressed with flamboyance and skill—and considerable expense—and he'd never seen her without make-up.

This girl looked as if she didn't know what make-up was. And her clothes...! Her clothes wouldn't be welcome at a welfare shop, he thought. They were dreadful.

But he could still see the resemblance—both to Fiona and to the little boy by her side.

And he remembered what the little boy had said. 'Gemma, I'm thirsty.' Not 'Mummy, I'm thirsty.'

'This is Fiona's child?'

'Good guess.'

'You don't want me to take him, too?' It was a harsh snap and she blinked. And then she smiled. Her arm came out and she hugged the little boy to her.

'No fear. Fiona was Cady's birth mother but I've been mother to him for over two years now. Cady and I are a team.'

They were, too. Woman and child against the world. He

stared at them both and they stared back—and again he felt his gut twist in a recognition of…

Of what? Of something. And he didn't know what the hell it was.

He took a grip on himself. Sort of. 'You're not prepared to take on a second?'

'No.'

'You'd better explain.'

Her chin jutted. 'I don't see why I need to.'

Heck, she couldn't just leave. She couldn't. What was she proposing—that she just set down the baby and walk away? The prospect made him feel dizzy. His world was tipping on its axis and he cautiously placed his hands flat down on the desk as if righting himself.

'I… Please.' Once more he forced his voice to steady. 'No, of course you don't need to. But…but I need to know. Everything.'

She stared at him for a long, long minute. And then she lifted the cup from her nephew's hands and set it on the desk.

'Cady, look. There's blocks in the corner,' she told him, motioning to where Nate kept a basket of toys to amuse small children. 'Can you build me a house?'

Cady considered and then nodded, with all the gravity of a carpenter agreeing to sign a contract for house construction.

'Sure.' He knelt on the floor and started to build. One block after another. The sight was somehow comforting compared to the unbelievable conversation that was taking place over the desk.

But then the doctor in him focused. The child seemed to be building more by feel than sight. He was lifting the coloured blocks and feeling their edges, fitting them together with a satisfactory click.

Was he blind? Maybe he normally wore glasses…

It wasn't his business. Cady wasn't his patient. Somehow this crazy conversation had to resume.

'Right,' Nate said. He took a deep breath and braced. 'Tell me.'

'My sister was… I think you could almost call her manic.'

'Now, that's what I don't understand.' Nate thought back to the last time he'd seen Fiona. Manic? For some reason the description suddenly seemed apt. He hadn't known why then. He didn't know why now.

'In what sense was she manic?'

'I told you she had diabetes.'

He thought that through and couldn't make sense of it. 'Diabetes is not usually a life sentence and it has nothing to do with a person's mental state.'

'It does if you're as perfect as Fiona.' Gemma shrugged. 'You need to understand. Fiona…well, she was two years younger than me and from the time she was born she was perfect. My mother certainly thought so. My mother was a beauty queen in her own right. My father left us before I can remember, and all my mother's pent-up ambitions centred on Fiona. Perfect Fiona.' She took a deep breath, fighting back bitterness that had been instilled in her almost since birth.

'Anyway, Fiona was as beautiful as even my mother could want. Even as a baby she was gorgeous and she turned from winning baby pageants to winning beauty contests almost without a break. And she was clever—brilliant really. She passed her exams with ease, she moved from one eligible man to another—whatever she wanted Fiona got. She was indulged to the point of stupidity by our mother, and when Mum died Fiona's boyfriends took right over.'

He saw. Or maybe he saw. 'And then?'

'And then she was diagnosed with type-one diabetes.'

'I don't understand.'

'Neither do I really. I only know that Fiona had just started medical school, she was flying high and suddenly she was faced with four insulin injections a day, constant monitoring and dietary restrictions.'

'I do know what diabetes is,' he told her. 'Type one... It's a damnable pest but if it's well controlled it's hardly life-threatening.'

'Hers wasn't well controlled. Not because it wasn't possible to control it but because she wouldn't. She hated it. She refused to monitor herself. She gave herself the same amount of insulin every day regardless of what her blood sugars were and sometimes she didn't even do that. She refused to accept the dietary modifications. You need to understand. For once it was an area where she wasn't perfect and she couldn't bear it.'

He thought about that. He had diabetics in his practice who refused to take care of themselves and the results could be catastrophic. But...

'She was a doctor. She knew. With medical training she'd know what the risks were.'

'I think,' Gemma told him, slowly as if the words were being dragged out of her, 'I think my sister was a little bit crazy. She'd been indulged all her life. She was the golden girl and everyone treated her as if she was perfect. The thought of injections, the thought of not being able to eat everything she wanted and the thought of her body being less than perfect... Well, as I said, I think she was a little bit mad. It was as if she saw diabetes as a bar to her perfection and if she ignored it, it'd go away. Only as a doctor you'd know that that's a disaster.'

He was horrified. Why hadn't he guessed any of this? He'd never even known she'd been diabetic. And not to control it... 'That's practically suicide.'

'Yes.' She gave a grim little nod. 'It is—and by the time she'd finished medical school the effects were starting to show. Then our mother died. Mum and Fiona had fought about Fiona's diabetic management. Fiona had rebelled but Mum's death just seemed to make things worse. Things weren't going right in Fiona's world and she reacted with anger. Her specialist told her that if she couldn't keep her diabetes under control then at least she shouldn't get pregnant. She must have been pregnant within minutes of him saying that. With Cady.' She shrugged and her eyes seemed to shadow with remembered pain. 'And her decision to have Cady tore our lives apart.'

Our lives? There was a desperate bleakness in her words and she looked as though she was staring back into a chasm that she couldn't quite escape.

'And?' Nate prodded, and Gemma seemed to shake herself back to reality. To the harshness of now. Her voice became brisk and carefully businesslike.

'And she darn near died having him. When she didn't it was as if she was mad at the world. As if she'd been cheated. She was furious that she didn't die and from then on she was on a downhill spiral of neglect.'

By now Nate was thoroughly confused. He shook his head, trying to reconcile what he was hearing with the vibrant, lovely doctor who'd swept into his life twelve months ago. 'She seemed fine. I didn't get any of this when she was here.'

'No.' She met his look, her eyes steady and challenging. 'I guess you only saw what most men saw—the gorgeous Fiona. Fiona the irresistible. But there was another Fiona— the Fiona who walked a fine line between sanity and madness. She had Cady and she walked away from him. She knew...she knew that I'd take care of him. How could I not? But I kept working. After what she'd done to me... I barely managed it but there were glimmers of my former life left.'

He still didn't follow. 'That sounds as if she was angry with you.'

'Of course she was.'

'I don't understand.'

'She was supposed to be the perfect one,' Gemma said wearily. 'And she was. My mother loved her to distraction and I was sidelined. But she was jealous even of that. She was jealous of me from the moment she was born—as if I could ever compete with her. It was crazy, but like a cuckoo in another bird's nest she'd push aside any sibling that competed for her attention. And when our mother got sick she leaned on me. That drove Fiona crazy—that Gemma, the plain one, should now have what she wanted. Health. And our mother's dependence. So she fixed me right up. She saddled me with a baby and then...and then when I managed to cope and still have a life—of sorts— she gave me another. And she died doing it.'

Dear heaven...

Nate sat back in his chair. He let what she'd said drift slowly though his mind, trying to assimilate it. He raised his hand and ran his fingers through his thatch of burnt-red curls, fighting for some sanity. Fighting for some reason.

'I don't know what to say,' he said at last. 'I can't think.'

'There's not much to think about.'

'Well, that's a crazy statement,' he snapped, shock giving way to anger. 'Not much to think about! When you come in here and present me with the fact that I'm a father...'

'If you slept with Fiona you must have known fatherhood was a possibility.'

'Of course I didn't.'

'You're a doctor,' she snapped back, as angry as he was. 'You know very well that no contraceptive is perfect. Unless it's abstinence. And you and Fiona didn't practise abstinence.'

'No, but—'

'But nothing. She's your baby.' She rose again and proffered her bundle. 'Are you going to take her—or are you intending to arrange an adoption? Fiona had this baby to punish me for not being ill. I've thought it through. It worked with Cady. I've taken him in and I've cared for him and I love him to bits. But with Mia…every time I look at her I get angry. That's no way to rear a child, Dr Ethan. She deserves better than that. So…you're her daddy. Will you take her—or will you find someone else who'll love her?'

He did have an option, he thought incredulously. He could just say take her away and she would. She'd hand her over to adoptive parents.

But no. She was way ahead of him.

'Don't even think about it,' she told him flatly, and it was as if she had read his mind. 'I'm not arranging the adoption. For a start that'd mean taking care of her for longer—and I daren't take the chance that I'll grow to love her. And even if I wanted to, I can't. There are no official documents naming me as her parent. There's only the birth certificate. Cady's birth certificate…well, Cady's certificate landed me right in it, but Mia's certificate says her mother is deceased and her father is Nate Ethan. You. So as of this moment you're her sole guardian. Like it or not.'

Carefully, deliberately, she set the sleeping baby on the desk in front of him.

She'd been well cared for, Nate saw in some deep recess of his brain that could still note such things. She was rosy and chubby and beautifully dressed. She'd been loved.

'How…how old did you say she was?'

'Four weeks. She should be smiling soon.'

'And…how long since Fiona…?'

'Fiona never regained consciousness after the birth. She lapsed into a coma at thirty-eight weeks and the doctors performed an emergency Caesarean. It was all horribly too late. She died the day after delivery.'

He closed his eyes. This was all far too much to take in. Fiona dead?

And he had a daughter.

No! 'You can't leave her here!'

'Watch me.' She tilted her chin in a gesture of defiance and then handed over a business card. 'This is where you can find me.'

'If I need you?'

'No.' She shook her head. 'I'm tired of being needed, Dr Ethan. Cady needs me and that's all the responsibility I can handle. But if…in future…you want Cady to meet his half-sister…'

Hell. The future stretched before him, vast and unknown. Ten minutes ago his future had been the Terama Jazzfest. Now…

'You can't do this.'

'I can.' She leaned over the little boy and took Cady's hand in hers. 'That's a great tower,' she told the little boy. 'But we need to go.'

'You're leaving town?' Nate's voice was an incredulous croak and she smiled, not without sympathy.

'That's the plan. We live in Sydney and it's a long drive.'

'But what the hell am I meant to do?'

'What I've been doing,' she told him. 'Shoulder your responsibility. You are a doctor after all. I assume you know baby basics and I've checked your background. You have a nice little bush nursing hospital on hand. They'll have everything you need.' She laid a bag on the desk beside the sleeping baby. 'This contains formula, bottles, clothes—everything you need. And now, Dr Ethan, you're on your own.'

But he wasn't on his own. Not quite.

From Reception there was the sound of a door opening and then closing, followed by brisk heels tapping across the floor. He'd left the door open just a little. Hannah, his receptionist, had seen his last patient for the day into his rooms and then left. There was no one out there. Except...

The door opened just a little and Donna's beautiful face peeked around.

'Yoohoo. Anyone home?' Her eyes found Nate and she smiled her loveliest smile. 'Nate, darling, we're going to be very late. I've brought your evening clothes so you can change here and we can get going right now.'

Compared to Fiona, Donna didn't cut it, but that didn't mean she wasn't gorgeous. She was tall, five feet eleven or so, willow thin and beautifully groomed. In fact, she was just the way Nate liked his women. And she was dressed to kill. She was wearing a 1920s costume—a pencil-thin fringed dress which accentuated every gorgeous curve as it shimmered and swayed, and high, high stilettos. Her sleek chestnut bob was adorned with a tiny velvet headband and feather, and she wore beads that reached almost to her hips.

She was some sight! Normally Nate would have whistled his appreciation. But he wasn't in the mood for whistling.

And Donna should have known better than to barge in on a patient.

'Donna, I'm busy.'

'No. No, he's not busy. Not any more.' Gemma smiled at the sight of Nate's girlfriend and held out her hand in welcome. 'This makes it all perfect. You have a new lady in your life. From what Fiona told me about you I was sure you wouldn't let grass grow under your feet. How do you do? I'm Gemma. And this is Cady. We're just leaving. But...' She eyed Donna's stunning dress with a wry smile.

'If I were you, I'd put a cloth over your shoulder if you're intending nursing Mia in that dress. She does suffer a little from reflux.'

With that she gave them both her very brightest smile, collected Cady and walked out the door.

'Stop!'

She didn't.

And Nate moved. Hell, he moved. He'd never moved faster in his life. Gemma had walked out into the reception area but before she could reach the door to the car park he was in front of her, blocking her path.

'You're not going anywhere.'

She raised her mobile eyebrows at that. 'You're planning on locking me up and throwing away the key?'

'No.'

'Then what?'

What? He ran his fingers though his hair and he groaned. 'Hell.'

'What's wrong, Nate?' Donna was clearly puzzled.

'I…this lady…Gemma…wants to leave me with her baby.'

'No.' Gemma wasn't having any of that. 'She's your baby. Not mine. Get things right.'

'Your baby.' Donna blenched. 'Yours! Did you and…?' She looked wildly from Gemma to Nate and back again, and Gemma gave a derisory laugh.

'Don't get yourself in a state here. No, Nate and I didn't do a thing. I've only just met your Dr Ethan. This isn't my baby. I'm only the stork, delivering his bundle whether he likes it or not.'

Donna's confusion grew. 'What's going on?'

What was going on? Nate didn't have a clue. He was so at sea that he felt like he was drowning. 'I don't know.'

'Let me past.' Gemma's voice was implacable.

'You can't leave.'

'I can. I must. I need to work tomorrow. I've taken every one of my sick days and more over the last few weeks, and if I'm not back tomorrow I risk being sacked.'

'You work?'

'Amazing but true.'

'And who looks after Cady while you work?'

'There's no joy down that road,' she snapped, seeing where his thoughts were headed. 'Cady goes to day care at the hospital and I can't afford to keep two children in care.'

'You're a nurse?'

'No, Dr Ethan.' Her patience had pretty much come to an end. 'I'm a doctor. Amazing as it sounds. Just like my sister. Only I'm so unlike my sister that you wouldn't believe it. In fact, I've never had an illegitimate child in my life. Now, if you don't mind...'

'Gemma, I feel funny.' The child's voice from beside her was neither plaintive or high-pitched. He was simply stating a fact, and Gemma closed her eyes in a gesture of sheer weariness.

'I know, sweetheart. So do I. I need to find somewhere for us to have dinner.' She turned back to Nate. 'I've been waiting all afternoon to see you and I can wait no longer. You have a baby to see to. I have Cady. So can we leave it, please?'

He stared down at the card that she'd given him. There it was in black and white. Dr Gemma Campbell. Anaesthetist. Sydney Central Hospital.

She really was a doctor.

And this was no nightmare. This was cold, hard fact.

'I can find you at Sydney Central?'

'Yes. As I said—only if you want the kids to be in contact. It's up to you. I'll tell Cady about Mia as he grows up, but if you don't want her to know...or if you decide on adoption...'

'Nate, honey, what the hell is going on?'

'It seems I have a baby,' Nate said in a voice that held not the slightest hint of humour. His tone said that he'd been trapped. There was anger behind the words and both women heard it.

And surprisingly Gemma's face softened into very real sympathy.

'I'm sorry, Nate,' she told him. 'I understand you've been used. But...so have I. And it does boil down to the fact that you're Mia's father. Good luck with her, and I hope you learn to love her—as I love Cady.'

And she smiled and walked around him. Out into the car park. Out of his life. For ever?

CHAPTER TWO

DONNA wasn't the least bit interested in babies.

'She has to be joking,' she said flatly as Gemma disappeared into the night. 'She can't just dump you with the kid.'

'No.'

But it seemed she had. Nate stared at the closed door, trying to figure out a reason why he should stride after her and stop her going. Could he ring the police? Could he have them haul her back and accept her responsibility?

But her conversation played itself back in his mind. Over and over. This baby wasn't Gemma's responsibility. She was Nate's.

One stupid act...

He should never have slept with Fiona, he thought wildly. Was he as crazy as Fiona had been? One stupid act...

'Nate, honey...'

'I don't think we're going to be able to go to the Jazzfest,' he told her, and her lovely face fell.

'But we must. We've had these tickets for ages and all our friends will be there.'

'Donna, leave it.'

She paused and stared at him. Then her eyes fell on the baby.

Mia was just waking, and her tiny eyelids fluttered open. With her eyes open the resemblance to Nate was almost uncanny.

'She really is your baby,' Donna whispered, stunned.

And Nate looked down.

Green eyes met green eyes. Her gaze was as intent and direct as his. Man and baby, meeting for the first time in both their lives.

Dear God… His gut wrenched as it had never been wrenched in his life before. She was just…beautiful. Perfect. Slowly he reached out a finger and traced the baby-soft skin of her cheek. Still her eyes held his, as if she knew that here was a man whose future was inexplicably locked to hers.

'You can't keep her.' Donna's voice sounded as if it were light years away—from a past life—and Nate had to wrench himself back to reality. To now. To here and to what counted for commonsense.

'I don't know.'

'The mother…'

'Is a past girlfriend. I didn't know she was pregnant. And now she's dead.'

'Oh, Nate, I'm sorry,' Donna said—with the easy sympathy of someone this didn't affect in the least. She glanced at her watch. 'Look, why don't we pop her over into children's ward? That way we can still make it to the Jazzfest in time for dinner.'

He thought that through. It had distinct appeal. What he needed desperately here was space. 'I suppose I could…'

'Of course you could. The nurses there are trained to take care of babies.' Donna's tone said that such things were unfathomable. Taking care of babies was something to be handled by experts. Like bomb detonation. 'And we don't want her to spoil our evening.'

'Donna, I—'

'Look, you're surely not suggesting we stay home and stare at a baby all night?'

He caught himself at that. It did seem ridiculous. And the hospital was quiet. There were places available in kids' ward.

He'd shelve the problem until tomorrow, he told himself. He'd give himself time to think.

'Maybe it's a good idea.'

'Of course it's a good idea.'

But as Nate lifted the tiny pink bundle into his arms—as he smelled the newborn milkiness of her and as he felt her nuzzle contentedly into his shoulder—he thought...

Stay at home and stare at a baby all night?

Suddenly it didn't seem such a crazy idea at all.

'My legs feel funny.'

Gemma bit her lip. She really had stretched Cady's patience to the limit. He was four years old, he was exhausted and he was very, very hungry.

She'd stretched him to the limit time and time again in the past few weeks, she thought bitterly. That was half the reason she was demanding that Nate take responsibility for Mia. Fiona had left a pile of bills a mile high. Gemma had needed to drop everything to be with her during the birth. And then afterwards—the funeral arrangements—everything had fallen to her. And all this time Cady had struggled uncomplainingly by her side.

She lifted him high into her arms and hugged him hard.

'It's over now, sweetheart. We're back to being just you and me.'

'I liked the baby.'

'I know. And she's your sister. When you get a bit bigger you'll be able to spend some time with her. I hope. But for now she's better off with her daddy. And I'm better off with you.'

'He was nice. I'd like a daddy like that.'

Yeah, right. As if. Gemma hugged harder as she carried the little boy into the roadhouse. The place was down at heel and looked distinctly seedy but its upside was that it also looked cheap. She could feed Cady enough to get them on the road back to Sydney.

He'd like a daddy like that?

She'd like one, too, she thought. She couldn't remember her own father. For the last few years her mother had leaned on her, and the responsibilities for Fiona had all been hers.

And Alan was still there—a nightmare in her background.

Sometimes the responsibilities were far, far too much.

'Let's just concentrate on food,' she told Cady. 'One step at a time.'

'Why can't he be our daddy?'

Because he'd never look sideways at the likes of me, she thought bitterly. What man would? A woman encumbered with debt and child and responsibility up to her ears. And Alan...

Damn. To her horror she felt tears stinging the back of her eyes and she blinked them back with a fierceness that surprised her.

She must be more exhausted than she'd thought.

'We'll just get food and then we'll go,' she told him, and set him down at the first table she came to.

And he swayed.

'Cady...' Her hands came onto his shoulders to steady him. What was wrong? 'Are you OK?'

'N-no,' he whispered, and she had to stoop to hear him. 'Gemma, the room's doing funny things. My eyes are doing funny things. Make them stop.'

'Sure, we can keep her overnight.' Jane, the cheerful night charge nurse accepted Mia with easy equanimity. 'What's wrong with her?'

'As far as I know, nothing.'

'She's been abandoned,' Donna chirped in from behind.

She'd accompanied Nate across the road to the hospital and stood waiting—still bearing his dinner suit. 'And we need to go to the Jazzfest.'

'Of course you do. But…did you say abandoned?' And then Jane lifted away the blanket covering the baby's head and her breath sucked in with astonishment. Her eyes flew from the baby's head to Nate's and then back again.

Gemma was right. He'd never be able to disown this baby, Nate thought grimly. And the news would be from one end of the valley to the other by the morning. Dr Ethan's baby, abandoned in Terama.

'Just look after her for me for the night,' he told Jane wearily. 'I need to sort out a few things—in the morning.'

'I'd imagine you do.'

His eyes flashed anger. 'There's no need to jump to conclusions.'

'No?' Jane was in her mid-forties. Nate was thirty-two so Jane was certainly not old enough to be his mother— but she sure acted like it.

'No!'

'Whatever you say, Dr Ethan.' She hugged the baby close. 'Oh, aren't you just delicious? Looking after you will be pure pleasure.' She waved Nate and Donna away. 'Off you go, and enjoy yourselves. And then come back to one gorgeous baby.'

How the hell was he supposed to enjoy himself after that?

Nate somehow managed to respond to his friends and he tried to eat his dinner but only half his mind was on what he was doing. Or less. Maybe less than ten per cent of his mind. The rest was back in the children's ward with a baby called Mia.

And maybe…maybe part of his mind was travelling up the highway toward Sydney, with one very weary doctor called Gemma and a little boy called Cady.

Oh, for heaven's sake, he couldn't worry about them. He had enough to worry about with Mia.

His daughter.

The knowledge went round and round his heart, insidious in its sweetness.

He should be panic-stricken, he thought, and a part of him was. The other...the other part remembered how his tiny daughter had felt snuggling into his chest. The way her fingers had curled around his. The feel of her soft curls under his chin...

Mia. His daughter.

And Gemma...

She was still in his thoughts. Try as he might, he couldn't stop thinking about her. She'd looked too damned tired to face the highway to Sydney.

He should have insisted she stay the night.

She'd be sacked if she stayed. What had she said? She'd used all her sick-pay entitlements and then some.

She'd taken on so much!

He could guess how it had been, he thought grimly. She'd coped with the responsibilities of a dying sister and her two children.

She'd handed over one. He should be angry.

He couldn't be angry. Whenever he tried, he kept thinking back to the feel of Mia against his chest and the anger dissipated, to be replaced by something that was akin to wonder.

He had a daughter.

And finally he could bear it no longer. He pushed away his half-finished plate of food and gave Donna an apologetic smile.

'I'm sorry, Donna, but I need to go.'

She was astonished. 'But you haven't been called and the dancing hasn't even started.'

'I need to go back to kids' ward.'

'To the baby?'

'To the baby. Yes.' He took a deep breath and accepted reality. 'To my baby.'

She stared at him in amazement. 'You're not going to keep it?'

'If I can. Yes. I think so.'

Her lovely eyes widened in astonishment. 'You surely can't be serious?' And then another thought hit her. 'You don't expect me to help, do you?'

'No, Donna, I don't expect that.'

'I don't think I'd be very good with babies.'

'That's fine.'

'And you really want to go?' Her lips pouted in displeasure. 'Go on, then. If you must. There's plenty of other men to dance with and to take me home.'

He knew that. Damn, he knew.

Maybe he was being stupid. He wavered, just for an instant, and in that instant the buzzer sounded on his belt. He lifted his cellphone and saw who was calling. The hospital charge nurse.

'Jane?'

'Nate, you'd better come. I need you here now.' She sounded rushed and that was all she had time for. The phone went dead before he learned any more.

Mia? Was there something wrong with Mia? His feet were taking him out the door before his phone had been clipped back on his belt. What was wrong?

When he had a call there was always tension—but not like his.

His daughter…

But it wasn't his daughter. It was Cady.

'I don't know what's wrong.' Gemma was beside herself. She was sitting in Emergency looking as sick as the child in her arms. 'He's just… Nate, he's hardly conscious.

I thought it was weariness but this is much more than weariness.'

Nate was still in his dinner suit. He looked handsome—absurdly handsome—but Gemma didn't notice. She didn't see Nate the man. She saw Nate the doctor, and the doctor was what she needed most at this moment. A doctor with skills. Please…

'Tell me what happened.' Nate's voice was curt and decisive, cutting through her fear. Or trying to. She might be a doctor herself but this was her beloved Cady and her medical judgement couldn't surface through her terror.

Somehow she forced herself to be calm. To give Nate the facts.

'We stopped a few miles down the road. I wanted to get a little distance between us…between the baby and us…before we ate. And Cady was really, really quiet but I thought, well, it was his little sister we'd just left. And we'd grown so fond… Regardless of what I told you…'

She was almost incoherent, Nate thought. She was hugging the little boy to her as she spoke and their faces were a matching chalky white. Jane had pressed Gemma into a chair and was taking Cady's blood pressure. She'd called Nate as soon as she'd seen Cady. The dance hall was only a few hundred yards from the hospital so he'd arrived there in minutes.

Nate listened to the fear in Gemma's voice. He stooped before them, lifting the boy's wrist and feeling his racing pulse. His breathing was deep and gasping—as if it hurt.

'OK, Cady, we'll have you feeling better in no time,' he told the little boy, sensing the rigid fear in the child's body. Obviously there were things happening that Cady didn't understand.

Neither did Gemma. 'OK, Gemma, just take it slowly,' he told her. 'Calm down.' His voice insisted she do just that. 'Tell me what happened next.'

She hiccuped on a sob. 'He said he couldn't see. He said everything was fuzzy. And then...he was violently ill and now he's limp...'

'OK.' This could be a number of things. The tension of the past hour had fallen away now to be replaced with a different sort of tension. Nate was back in medical mode and nothing else mattered. What was happening here? What did he have? One limp kid?

Meningitis? Maybe it was, and he could tell by the fear in Gemma's voice that that was what she was terrified of.

Okay. Worst case scenario first. Rule of thumb—look for the worst and work backwards.

'There's no temperature,' Jane told him, showing him the thermometer. 'High blood pressure. Rapid pulse. But no temp.'

OK. Breathe again. That should rule out meningitis.

But Cady certainly looked sick.

The child was thin, Nate thought, sitting back on his heels and really looking. Taking his time. He'd learned in the past that unless airways were threatened, such examinations were important. So he took the child in from head to toe—examining him with his eyes instead of his hands.

What did he have?

Thin child. Fuzzy vision. Sick. Tired, and drifting into semiconsciousness.

Diabetic mother...

And a little voice was recalled from nowhere. The memory slammed home.

'Gemma, I'm thirsty.'

Click.

'Jane, I want a blood sugar,' he said curtly. He put his hand over Cady's and gripped, hard. 'Cady, your eyes are a bit funny, are they? Can you hear me, Cady? Can you tell me what's happening?' The little boy seemed as if he was drifting in and out of consciousness.

'I can't... Everything looks funny.' Cady's voice was a bewildered whisper and Nate's eyes met Gemma's. The child's confusion was reflected in hers.

'Cady, I'm going to take a tiny pinprick of blood,' he told the little boy. 'Not much. It'll be a tiny prick. I think you might have too much sugar in your blood and I want to find out if I'm right. If that's what's making you sick.'

'Oh, no...' Gemma's voice was so distressed he could tell she was near breaking point, but she'd realised where he was headed. Blood sugar... 'Of course,' she whispered, distressed beyond measure. 'How can I have been so stupid...? It'll be ketoacidosis.'

Diabetic ketoacidosis.

Nate thought it through, but the more he thought the more it fitted with what was happening. Diabetes meant the pancreas stopped producing insulin—and if insulin wasn't available the body couldn't absorb food and started using its own fat for energy. The result was a poisonous accumulation of ketones. Ketoacidosis. And in its early stages ketoacidosis looked just like this.

'We don't know yet,' he told her.

But Jane was moving as he spoke, fetching the equipment he needed. A urine sample would check for ketones, but taking a urine sample from Cady now would be difficult. So he'd test the blood sugar and assume the rest.

The sugar reading took seconds. He took a drop of blood from the little boy's listless hand, placed it on the testing strip and set the machine in motion.

And five seconds later there was the answer.

'Thirty-two...'

They had their diagnosis.

'Dear God!' Gemma was rocking the little boy back and forth in her arms with anguish. Thirty-two! She knew all too clearly what that meant. A normal range was from four to eight. No wonder his vision was blurred. No wonder he

was sick. 'He's diabetic. Dear God... How could I not
have known? How could I not have guessed?'

'You've had just a bit on your mind lately,' Nate said
gently. She certainly had, and here was another load for
her to bear. What on earth had her sister landed her with?
'But let's not worry. Let's just get Cady feeling better. I
need to ring a specialist paediatrician for some up-to-date
advice but I think I can handle this here.' He smiled down
at the bewildered Cady. Even though he wasn't sure
whether the little boy could hear him he spoke anyway,
and maybe it was more for Gemma than for Cady.

'Cady, there's something in your tummy called a pancreas. It isn't doing its job so we'll have to fix that. The
pancreas makes stuff called insulin that keeps you well,
and because your pancreas isn't making any insulin I'm
going to pop a tube into your arm so we can give you
some.' Heaven knew if the child could make sense of this.

But Cady was one brave kid and he was trying. He was
struggling to focus on Nate's face but it was beyond him.
'Will it hurt?' he quavered, and Gemma hugged him tight
and kissed him on the top of his head.

'It'll be a small prick just like the last one—and it'll
make you feel so much better,' she told him. He'd need a
drip, she knew. They had to get some nourishment into
the child to stop the deadly breakdown of body fat and
they'd need intravenous insulin to get the blood-sugar level
down. 'Dr Ethan will pop a tube into your hand so the
medicine can go in really quickly.' There were myriad
blood tests to be done but the blood could be taken as the
IV line was put in. 'Then we'll pop you in bed and let you
sleep, Cady. For just as long as you need to sleep to be
well again.'

'You won't be taking him back to Sydney any time soon.'
'I know.' With Cady safely tucked into a ward bed

Gemma seemed to have lost the last of her energy. She slumped forward on her chair, her shoulders sagging and her whole body spelling defeat. 'I almost killed him.'

'You did no such thing.'

'I'm a doctor.' She was very close to tears, Nate thought. She was very close to breaking down altogether. 'I should have noticed. Of all the stupid...'

'You know as well as I do that diabetes is insidious,' he said gently. 'He'll have been eating and doing everything he normally does... There are no overt signs.'

'But he's thin. I thought... I thought he was just having a growth spurt.'

'And you were taken up by a dying sister and a newborn baby.'

'I let it go so far. I could have killed him.'

'No!' He stooped and took her shoulders and gripped, hard. 'You didn't. Diabetes in children is hard to pick before it becomes an acute problem. You think a kid's having a growth spurt—they're suddenly taller and thinner and tired, and you put two and two together and get four—but the answer's six. I've seen this before, Gemma.'

'As bad as this?'

'Worse.' His hands still gripped her too-thin shoulders. Did she have any time to look after herself? he wondered. And then he thought... What was her blood sugar?

'Can we test you?' he asked, and she gave a laugh that was almost hysterical.

'I'm not diabetic.'

'How do you know?'

'I...' She took a grip. 'I guess I don't. But I'm not thirsty like Cady. And I'm not losing weight.'

'You mean you've always been this thin?'

'I eat on the run,' she told him. 'But Cady...'

'Will be fine.'

'His body must have been producing ketones for weeks.'

'Kids get sick fast,' he told her. 'It's my guess that further blood tests will tell us this is recent. You would have noticed if he'd been tired for months.'

'But not weeks. I've been so caught up—'

'With your sister and the baby.' He was still holding her. She hadn't noticed—or rather she had, but she needed the contact. She needed the warmth.

'I…' For the first time she seemed to surface. She shook herself like she was clearing fog and she looked at him. And saw Nathan for the first time. Really saw him.

'You're in a dinner suit,' she said stupidly, and he grinned. It really was the most gorgeous grin. It warmed places in her heart she hadn't known were cold.

'It's a bit more formal than a white coat,' he told her. 'I put it on for my favourite patients.'

There was an attempt at a smile. 'I've dragged you away from something.' And then her mind focused even more. 'Where's Mia?' Her voice cracked and his grip on her shoulders tightened.

'Hey, hang on. I haven't abandoned her.'

'Where is she?' She rose, and so did her voice.

'In the next cubicle,' he told her.

'You admitted her to hospital? Why? What's wrong?'

She was so close to the edge… 'Nothing's wrong,' he said flatly, checking the hysteria before it started. 'I had a date so I left her in kids' ward.'

'You had a date…'

'A jazz ball.' He motioned to his dinner suit. 'You see? The pieces of the jigsaw fit together.'

Gemma took a deep, searing breath and regrouped. But the anger didn't fade. 'You mean you went to a ball—and left Mia in hospital?' All the emotions of the last few weeks were contained within the fury of her voice. Nate saw anger surge and resurge. 'Of all the stupid, selfish, arrogant… You have a precious new daughter and you put her in hospital. In hospital! She's not sick. You know about Golden Staph. You know kids can get sick in hospital even if they're well to begin with. And she's yours. She's your daughter and you dump her—'

'Shush…'

'Don't shush me.' Her anger had built to boiling point. Her eyes were flashing fire. She took a step back and if looks could have killed, he'd have been dead on the floor right now. 'You toad. You uncaring, unfeeling, insensitive toad. You and Fiona. You're a type. Bring a baby into the world and then you don't give a toss. Hand her over to the nearest stupid person who'll take on your responsibilities—'

That was a bit much. 'Hey, Jane's not stupid.' He was nettled. After all, he'd handed Mia over to his most trusted nurse. 'And this is a tiny country hospital, Gemma. It's not a big city hospital where infections are a problem. Until Cady came in Mia was the only child in the kids' ward. Infections are hardly an issue. Touch wood, but we've never had a case of Golden Staph and, please, God, we never will. So.' He paused and his eyes met hers and held. Challenging. 'Any other complaints?'

He was smiling at her, she thought incredulously. The fink. He was smiling!

'You're laughing. How can you laugh?' Her anger was building even more, rather than waning. 'You have a baby and you just dump her…'

'Gemma…'

'Don't Gemma me.'

'Right.' His hands came out and caught her again and he held. Her whole body stiffened in his grasp—she was rigid with fury. She wrenched herself backward, but he was having none of it.

'I'm not as irresponsible as you think.'

'How the hell would you know what I think?'

He grinned at that. 'Maybe I can guess.'

'You know nothing. You and Fiona—'

'No.' He took her hands and gripped hard, forcing her to pause mid tirade. 'Let's get one thing straight, Gemma. I am not Fiona and there's been no me and Fiona. Fiona and I were a mistake. Apart from that one disastrous time, which I will regret for ever…'

'Because of Mia?'

That gave him pause. Because of Mia?

He thought of the baby as he'd last seen her, curled in sleep like a furled rosebud. She was the most beautiful, most perfect creature.

His daughter.

He'd hardly had time to get used to the idea. But… If he could undo what had gone before, wish away her existence… Would he?

There was uncertainty in his face and Gemma saw it. And she couldn't understand.

'But you left her,' she said flatly.

And Nate thought, How could I?

The Jazzfest. Donna.

Sanity.

'Yes. I left her.' He took a deep breath. 'Gemma, I have a life.'

'Well, bully for you.' Her voice cracked with tears. 'As opposed to me who gets to pick up the pieces of all these people who have *a life*.'

'Not tonight you don't,' he said flatly. Jane came back into the ward then, and she smiled at both of them as Nate looked at her questioningly. 'Are we organised?'

'Tony's in the kitchen, cooking, as we speak,' Jane told them. 'He was at the ball so he's just popped over to cook for you and will go back afterwards.'

'Tony?' Gemma was confused.

'Tony's the hospital cook,' Nate told her. 'My cooking skills are limited and I figured something more than a cheese sandwich was called for. Something tells me you've been running on cheese sandwiches—or less—for a long time. Now, I'm about to take your blood sugar just in case, and then we'll wrap you around a steak with the trimmings.'

'I don't want—'

'You know, I'm very sure you do.'

His tone was gentle and Gemma blinked. In the face of her fury he had the capacity to undermine her reason. She should turn on her heel and refuse to have anything to do with this man.

But he had just taken care of Cady with compassion, skill and kindness. She was stuck here at least until tomorrow and probably longer. Cady was in his hands—and so was Mia, long term.

'Let's go,' he told her. 'Eat and then let fly at me all you like. There's nothing like a good steak to fuel anger.'

She choked, but it was on something that might have passed for laughter. 'Oh, for heaven's sake…'

'That's better.' Nate smiled into her angry eyes and his smile was enough to counter anger all on its own. All of a sudden the thought flashed into her mind—I can see why Fiona chose him for the father of her baby.

What was she thinking? That was dangerous territory. She was here to hand over a baby and move on. Leaving her emotions absolutely intact.

'I'll be alright,' she said stiffly but he smiled again and took her shoulders, twisting her body away from his and propelling her out the door.

'Yes, Dr Campbell. You'll be fine. Just as soon as you've had something to eat. Jane will watch over Cady for us and let us know if he so much as blinks. If he needs you, we'll come. But meanwhile you have needs as well. For now, Dr Campbell, just shut up and let yourself indulge in what you need. *You.'*

'But—'

'Not another word.' And he grinned down at her, that dangerous, laughing smile that made her heart do strange things inside her chest. 'Let's go. Now.'

He wouldn't listen to another word.

He sat on the other side of the big kitchen table and traded easy laughter with Tony, a beefy Irishman with a twinkle and a flair for making the most mouthwatering steak and stir-fried vegetables that Gemma had ever eaten.

They were quite a pair, Gemma thought. The two men were both in dinner suits, Nate's well cut and smoothly black without adornment—with looks like Nate's who needed adornment? Tony's was the same with the addition of a vast green cummerbund, which made his not inconsiderable midriff seem huge.

And Nate was right. She was starving. The sight of food made her realise just how hungry she was. She was almost through her steak before she ventured to say a word and even then it was tentative.

'You've been very good... Both of you. And to leave the ball...'

'Think nothing of it.' Tony waved away her thanks with indifference. 'A man needs a break from all this capering, and the serious drinking's hardly started.'

'You'd still have had a good dinner if you'd arrived at three in the morning,' Nate told her. 'But the sauce would be a bit more alcoholic. Burgundy sauce is one of Tony's specialities but the later in the evening it is, the more burgundy it contains.'

'Hey, don't scoff at my gravy. It's a recipe handed down from generation to generation. My old granny—'

'Who died of alcoholic poisoning aged a hundred...'

'She did nothing of the sort,' Tony said with dignity. 'She didn't die. Aged a hundred, we were able to bury her pickled and preserved for posterity.'

And so they continued, bantering easily above Gemma's head while the wonderful food slipped down, the warmth of the kitchen enveloped her and a feeling of caring prevailed.

For some stupid reason there were tears welling behind her eyes. Why? Crying was something she'd sworn she was done with, yet today the tears were constantly threatening.

'The lady's asleep in her dinner,' Tony said gently and Gemma forced her head up and her eyes wide.

'No, I—'

'I'll take you to bed,' Nate told her, and Tony laughed. 'Now, there's a dangerous line.'

It certainly was. Gemma's eyes were wide now and she was awake. Sort of.

'I... I'll go back to Cady.'

Nate shook his head. 'There's no need. You know as well as I do that Cady will sleep until morning.'

'But—'

'And if he doesn't...' Nate said gently, rising and coming around the table to her side. She rose and staggered—the warmth and the weariness proving too much—and his arm came around her shoulders and held. As if he cared. 'If he doesn't and he needs you then Jane will come and find you. But for now, you're coming with me.'

'No.'

'You needn't think my plans are underhand,' he told her, but his smile suggested just that and more. 'I have a feeling sleeping with you would be just that. You're asleep on your feet already. No. The doctors' quarters adjoin the hospital and Cady will be a door away. We have a spare bedroom and a spare bed. What do you say, Dr Campbell? Wouldn't you like to fall into bed?'

No.

Yes!

And suddenly to do anything else was unthinkable. Both men were looking at her, smiling in compassion and caring, and those damned tears were threatening to well and to fall.

She had no choice.

'Yes, please,' she told them with as much dignity as she could muster.

'Yes!'

And before she could protest the arm around her shoulders dropped and she was swept up into a pair of strong, warm arms. Laughing eyes danced down at her. Her feeble protests were ignored and Gemma Campbell, anaesthetist, independent career-woman—and total wuss—was carried straight to bed.

CHAPTER THREE

Two a.m. Time for sleeping. But Nate wasn't asleep. He'd tossed and turned for a couple of hours and then thrown back the covers and taken himself through the adjoining door into the hospital.

All was quiet. There were only four patients in the little bush nursing hospital—four patients plus Cady and Mia. And there were no problems tonight. Everyone seemed to be sleeping. Nate made his way through to kids' ward and Jane was there, sitting beside Cady. When the nurse saw him she smiled and rose.

'They're both fine. I've just taken Cady's blood pressure and sugar levels and he didn't stir. You want to see?' She handed over the chart.

Twenty. His sugar level was dropping already. Good. It looked good. He gazed down at the sleeping child and he thought, Hell, what a diagnosis. It was so unfair.

But at least this was the twenty-first century, he thought thankfully. Fifty years ago this diagnosis would have meant major health problems. Now, as long as Cady was careful with himself, there was no reason to think he couldn't look forward to a long and eventful life.

But he'd still have to cope with insulin injections. Maybe medical researchers would develop a constant infusion mechanism, he thought, to halt the need for constant injections. Or a cure. Soon…

'Nate, he'll be fine,' the nurse said, watching his face and obviously puzzled by his reaction. 'Kids take to diabetes really easily—much more so than adults. My nephew's diabetic and he lectures me about good and bad foods all the time.'

'Yes. I know.'

Still she was watching him with curiosity. There was a lot going on here that Jane didn't understand.

But she did understand one thing.

'Your daughter needs feeding.' There was a vague whimpering from behind the partition. Mia was stirring and her whimpering was threatening to build to a full-throated roar. But not yet. She was simply letting them know it was time.

'Do you want to feed her?'

'No, I—'

'I'll prepare the formula,' she told him, disregarding his refusal as if he hadn't made it. 'You change her nappy.'

'Me…?'

'You have to start some time—Daddy.' And she grinned and headed to the kitchen before he could say another word.

His daughter.

Mia was his daughter.

Somehow Nate changed her nappy—a thing he would have thought impossible. There was nothing to it, he thought as he adjusted the tapes. He lifted her from the change table feeling smug.

Her nappy fell to the floor.

Whoops.

'OK, young lady, let's try again.'

The second attempt was no better than the first but he had the sense not to pick her up straight off. He wrapped her up in her bunny rug before lifting her and when he picked her up he carried her horizontally back to his chair.

Miraculously the nappy stayed put. Great. Well done,

he thought, and his chest expanded a notch or two with paternal pride. Nothing to this parenting caper...

Now what? He'd hauled on jeans and a T-shirt before he'd come into the hospital and it had been a good choice. His T-shirt was soft and warm, and the baby nestled in as if she belonged. Her tiny rosebud mouth puckered as she turned her cheek, searching for a teat.

'It's coming,' he told her. Jane entered with Mia's bottle and he looked up at her and smiled. 'Just in time. She looks as if she's planning a riot.'

'They're good at getting what they want.' And she handed him the bottle.

'Aren't you—?'

'She's not a patient,' Jane said softly. 'She's your daughter. Your baby. You feed your baby, Dr Ethan. From this day forth...'

Gemma woke and it was still dark. For a moment she couldn't think where she was and then the events of the previous day flooded back.

Cady...

She'd just check.

By the glimmer of moonlight streaming in across her bed she could see there was a gown of sorts hanging behind the door. Where was she, for heaven's sake? She'd been three-quarters asleep when she'd fallen into bed.

It wasn't worth taking her bearings now. The gown looked big and warm—in fact, it fell all the way to the floor and would have wrapped around her twice. She snuggled into it and made her way through the darkened house to the hospital next door.

Nate was there.

For a moment she thought she was dreaming. She opened the door of kids' ward and there he was.

He was settled into an easy chair beside the crib, and

he was holding his baby daughter in his arms. The over-head light was off. Only a dim night-light shone beside the chair.

But it was enough to see him by. And the look on his face...

It made her catch her breath in sheer astonishment.

He hadn't heard her. He was intent only on the baby in his arms. Mia was nearing the end of the bottle, sated with milk, warmth and the security of a baby who knew that everything in her life was right.

And why shouldn't it be? Gemma thought, dazed. That such a man should hold her. And love her...

It might just work, she thought incredulously. Nate was looking down into his daughter's tiny face with such a look of wonder and awe...

It was as if he'd been granted a miracle.

She would have tiptoed away. If she could have. But Cady was beyond him, through the partition separating babies from children. She took a step forward and Nate looked up and saw her.

'Gemma?'

He sounded as surprised as she was—and maybe he was. She must look a sight. This was some crazy dressing-gown. It was made of quilted velvet—vast and luxurious and totally over the top. She felt like she had an insect-sized head on a vast crimson body.

'Um...sorry. I was just checking on Cady.'

He didn't move. How could he? He was holding his daughter.

'Cady's fine,' he told her. 'His sugar's down past twenty. The saline drip's being running for six hours now so he'll have fluids aboard. The worst is over.'

The worst is over... Gemma let that sink in. The enormity of it.

The last four weeks had been hell. Culminating in tonight. She walked around the partition, looked down at Cady's sleeping face and thought, Is it true?

Is the worst over?

Maybe. And if Nate could learn to love his daughter...

She'd only have one responsibility. Only Cady. And with Cady she could cope.

She loved him so much. She closed her eyes and trouble flooded back. The thought of tomorrow. Of saving her job. Of facing Alan with this further drain on her salary. He'd known she was bringing Mia here and he'd approved, but she should be back in Sydney now.

If she lost her job he'd be furious, and with good reason.

But how could she cope? Would the child-care centre take Cady back, knowing that he was a diabetic?

She'd resign and take care of him—but if she lost her job, Alan would—

'Worry about tomorrow tomorrow,' Nate said gently, and she jumped. Heck, what was it about the man? Did he have a crystal ball?

'I'm not—'

'You're worrying about the future. One day at a time, Gemma. Or one night. And speaking of nights, you have no business being awake. I put you to bed.'

'I'm not very good at staying put.'

'I can see that.' Nate rose and stood looking down at her, his tiny daughter cradled in his arms. 'But there are no problems tonight. I'm in charge. And look,' he told her, and there was a huge amount of pride in his voice, 'I've fed her, I've changed her nappy and I've put her back to sleep.'

'That's wonderful.' And it was. Gemma smiled up at him, their smiles caught and held—and all of a sudden the room was full of something she didn't understand.

What?

It was like an electric charge. Her body felt weird—

tingly—strange, and Nate's eyes were warming her from the toes up.

When finally she found her voice it came out wrong. Like a breathless whisper. Which was stupid.

'Um…maybe I'd best go back to bed.'

'Maybe you had.' He grinned but the tiny flicker of uncertainty behind his eyes told her that he'd felt it, too. Whatever it was. 'Don't worry about me,' he told her. 'I'm coping brilliantly. Superdad, that's me.'

And as he lifted his daughter toward her crib one small nappy hit the floor.

Dawn found Nate wide awake, waiting for eight o'clock. Waiting until he could make a few phone calls to Sydney.

'If I'm not back tomorrow I risk being sacked.'

He remembered what Gemma had said when she'd been facing the long drive back to Sydney. That alone warranted a phone call but Nate hesitated before making it, thinking it through. There was an idea germinating in his head. A way out of this mess. Maybe…

First things first. Gemma had to be a better doctor than her sister, he thought, and any fool could tell that she was.

But he needed to check. Never again would he risk patients' lives by employing someone without thorough checking. He'd employed Fiona on the basis of written testimonials and fantastic academic results and look where that had landed him. So instead of ringing Gemma's direct boss he found himself ringing a friend of his. He'd trained with Jeff. Jeff was a pathologist based at Sydney Central and the hospital wasn't *that* big. He must know Gemma.

He did. Jeff's response was direct and filled with warmth. 'Gemma. Of course I know Gemma. What the hell's she doing down there?'

Nate told him and there was a long silence on the end of the line.

'Poor kid. Is there no end to her troubles? And Margot will have kittens,' he said at last. 'Hell.'

'Margot being Gemma's boss?'

'That's the one. I could put you through to let you explain but I don't like your chances of keeping Gemma's job open until she gets back. Margot's not one for suffering fools gladly.'

Nate frowned. 'Meaning Gemma's a fool.'

'Hell, no.' There was no hesitation there. 'There's no one I'd rather work with than Gemma. She's a fine anaesthetist—a fine doctor.'

'But Margot's attitude...'

'Margot couldn't stand the sister. Come to think of it, no one could—once they saw past that beautiful face. She was as mad as a cut snake and what she and that husband of hers did to Gemma...'

Husband? Fiona's husband? Nate was confused but Jeff continued without pausing for breath. He sounded indignant.

'They fed her a pack of lies. And she believed it. Hell, as far as I know, she still believes it. She won't talk about Fiona to anyone. And now she's dead. I still can't believe it. Of all the waste... Stupid cow.'

Nate was no longer sure who they were talking about—and he wasn't sure he wanted to know. Fiona's lurid background had nothing to do with him any more. Except for one baby...

'But Gemma's OK?'

'Gemma's great.' The indignation was replaced again with warmth. 'She works herself to death—burning the candle at both ends just trying to stay afloat—but she's a wonderful team member. When do you reckon she'll be back?'

'I guess that depends on Margot.'

'Well, good luck with that, mate,' Jeff said ruefully. 'I'll put you through but I warn you—hold your earpiece away from your ear or you'll risk a perforated eardrum.'

'Awake?'

If she hadn't been, she was now. Gemma opened her eyes and sat bolt upright, and she said the first thing that entered her mind.

'Cady.'

'Cady's fine.'

Nate's voice said she'd better believe him and she did. She closed her eyes and a shudder went right through her. And then she opened them.

She was in bed—and it was *some* bed. It was *some* bedroom.

She'd been so tired the night before that she'd fallen into bed without noticing, and her foray into the hospital had been done in the dark. But now... Daylight brought reality and reality was...well, wow!

The room was enormous, with a huge four-poster bed claiming pride of place in the centre of the room. There were high ceilings, vast, billowing curtains, a fireplace complete with glowing coals from the fire lit the night before—and wide French windows looking out to the veranda and down to the river beyond.

And between here and the river... There was a vast wing that looked like a conservatory but Gemma blinked and looked again as she saw through the huge wall of glass. It was a swimming pool! A magnificent indoor pool. She could see the steam rise gently from here and she thought, Wow!

This was the bedroom of dreams—the house of dreams— *and this was a doctors' residence?*

Well, this was certainly a doctor. Nate was watching her with amused eyes, and this morning he was all doctor. He was wearing a white coat over his casual jeans, and a stethoscope dangled erratically from his pocket.

Doctor at ease…

'Good morning,' he told her—and smiled. And she blinked.

What a smile! It was enough to make a girl forget about taking the next breath.

'Good morning,' she managed, and if her voice was feeble, well, who could blame her?

'Um… Have I died and gone to heaven?'

His grin deepened. 'It's great, isn't it?'

'I feel like I should at the very least be wearing a tiara.' She stared around her in deep appreciation. 'It's wonderful.'

'It is at that.'

'You did say it was the doctors' quarters.'

'We believe in living well.'

We…

Was he living with someone, then? The 1920s woman? Who Nate Ethan was living with was hardly important. Cady was important.

'You said Cady is fine?'

'I said Cady is fine. He's been awake, he's eaten a little breakfast, we have his sugar levels down to fourteen—still high, I know, but it's a vast improvement—and he's now asleep again.'

'But he woke.' Gemma's face creased in distress. 'And I wasn't there. You said you'd wake me…'

'If Cady needed you,' he finished for her. 'He slept right through the night, he stirred before Jane went off duty, she fed him herself and she cuddled him back to sleep. He's fine. He's a very self-assured young man.'

'He has to be,' she said, still distressed. 'He spends his time in a crèche. It's so unfair.'

'He's quite a kid.'

Her eyes flashed to his—checking to see if this was just politeness. Something he'd say to all his patients about their children. But it was no such thing. His eyes met hers and held, and she thought she could believe what this man said.

He liked Cady.

'I like him myself,' she told him, and he smiled.

'Is that why you took him on?'

She hesitated. 'I took him on because Fiona refused to have him adopted and refused to care for him. She knew I couldn't bear to see him neglected. She thought it'd finish my medical career, you see.'

He shook his head. 'No. I don't see.'

She shrugged. 'Maybe you don't have to. Fiona's jealousy of me was almost unbalanced. Or maybe I should say it was definitely unbalanced.'

'She was psychotic?'

'In a way—yes.' Then she glanced down at the clock on her bedside table and she started in dismay. 'Yikes!' She tossed back the covers—then she hauled them hastily back when she remembered what she was wearing. She'd gone to bed in her T-shirt and panties but she'd hauled off her jeans and she was scarcely respectable. 'Um…sorry.'

She must really look a sight, she thought ruefully, in her too-big T-shirt, with her black curls in a tangled mat around her shoulders and… And not much else.

But Nate was smiling. 'Think nothing of it,' he said magnanimously and his mischievous grin flashed out. 'I'll just think of you as a patient.'

'Yeah, right.' But her mind was moving on past his dangerous smile to the next problem. 'I can't believe it.'

'You can't believe what?'

'It's eight-thirty. Why didn't you wake me?'

'You needed to sleep as much as Cady did.'

'But now…'

'Now?'

She bit her lip, reality dawning with sick certainty. 'I was supposed to be at work at eight and I haven't even rung. I think I've just lost my job.'

'You have.'

Her eyes flew to his. 'What…?'

'I phoned,' he told her, and took the card she'd given him from his pocket. 'You told me—remember?—that you've already taken every one of your sick days and if you weren't back this morning you risked being sacked.'

'Yes, but—'

'So I thought I might do some good,' he told her. 'I figured if I rang in early and found your boss I could explain before she fired you.'

'You don't explain things to Margot.'

'I know that now. She's an appalling woman.'

'She's a dragon. She's unmarried and bitter as hell and she's never taken a day off sick in her life. She thinks women who do are wimps. And me… She thinks I'm the world's worst. She knew Fiona, you see, and she told me I should have let her rot rather than try to help. According to Margot, taking on the children was just ridiculous.'

'Did you explain that in coming down here you were trying to offload one of the children?'

'You talked to Margot,' Gemma said shortly. 'Do you think it's possible to explain anything to that woman?'

'Maybe not.' Nate hesitated, watching her face. 'She shouted at me, in fact. She said she'd reorganised your operating lists for the last time. That if you can't make it in by ten this morning then you needn't bother returning.'

'Great.' Gemma winced. In truth, she felt ill. The thought of the debts accumulating all the time was appalling and now she'd have Cady's medical bills to add to them.

Alan would have kittens…

'I can go above her if you like,' Nate suggested. She looked a real waif, he thought, sitting up in bed, hugging her knees, her deep black curls wisping over her eyes—the crazy red ribbon had given up the ghost and her curls were any which way. 'I have friends who are higher in the medical establishment than your Margot.'

'Yeah, right. So they'd get me my job back but I'd still have to work under Margot. Who's impossible.'

'That makes me feel better.'

'Sorry? Feel better about what?'

'About what I've done. You know, maybe it's not such a satisfactory job.'

'I know,' she said bitterly. 'But where else can I get on-site child care?'

'Here.'

Here.

The one syllable took her breath away. She stared in open-mouthed astonishment. But Nate didn't appear to notice.

'It's time to confess all,' he told her, with an expression that said he didn't feel guilty in the slightest about what he'd done. 'You didn't get the sack,' he told her. 'I saw which way the wind was blowing so you quit.'

He had her pole-axed. 'I quit?'

'It seemed the best thing to do. I could have told your dreadful boss that Terama was a five-hour drive from Sydney and that you had a snowball's chance in a bushfire of getting there by ten. But then she would have just said you were sacked. So I thought it was better that you leave on the high ground. I told her you felt her attitude made your continued employment untenable and that your resignation would be faxed through by lunchtime.'

'My resignation...' Gemma was almost speechless.

'Your resignation.' Nate smiled. 'You were quite uppity,' he told her. 'Talk about holding the moral high ground…'

'I was quite uppity?' Oh, great.

His smile faded. 'Gemma, there wasn't any choice. You know there wasn't.' He hesitated as he watched her face. He was assessing her gathering anger. But he forged on, regardless. 'I also rang a friend of mine who's a Sydney barrister. I explained the situation. And I played him the tape…'

By now she was thoroughly confused. Angry but confused. 'What tape?'

'I taped the conversation.'

'With Margot?'

'That's the one. I thought I'd better tape the conversation and I was right.' His cheerfulness reasserted itself—the man was incorrigible. 'And it's great. When I told her Cady had collapsed with ketoacidosis Margot said that had nothing to do with her—or your employment. Women who didn't keep their lives organised weren't welcome on her staff. In fact, doctors with young children were a damned nuisance and if she had her way she'd sack the lot of them. Given her attitude, your resignation was inevitable and the discrimination board will love it.'

'The discrimination board…' She was so confused she could hardly believe her ears.

But Nate wasn't confused in the least. He'd acted with ruthless purpose. 'That's right. Women with children have rights, too, you know. Mike—my lawyer mate—reckons the hospital will pay compensation so fast you won't be able to blink. The tape itself isn't admissible evidence but Mike knows—and the hospital administration knows—that it would severely embarrass them. He's onto it now. He says you'll have a cheque by the end of the month and if it's not equal to a year's salary or more, he'll eat his wig.'

'You're kidding,' she said faintly, and his smile blazed out in force.

'Nope. I don't kid about important things like this. So, can we move on?'

Move on? He'd just removed her pressing financial commitments. A year's salary...

She could stay home and care for Cady.

'You know, I don't actually see how being a stay-at-home parent will solve your problems,' he told her, and she blinked.

'How do you know what I'm thinking?'

'You have a very transparent face.'

Oh, great. The man really could read minds and the thought was frightening.

'Well, you're wrong,' she snapped crossly. 'It would solve my problems and I'd make a very good stay-at-home mum. Cady needs me so much.'

'And... Let me see. It's my guess you have a tiny hospital apartment?'

'Yes, but—'

'Now you're no longer a hospital employee you'll have to move. And without a crèche... Can you find playmates for Cady? Do you have many friends outside work?'

She caught her breath. 'No. But I can find some.'

'After you've found somewhere else to live.'

She started to snap back—and then she paused. He was right. She'd have to leave the hospital, and city apartments were expensive. Maybe if she looked in the outer suburbs she could find something. The thought was daunting.

'Um... I don't think I can afford much...'

'What about this place?'

Here we go again. He was moving so fast he was taking her breath away. She stared at him across the room, then hauled her bedding up to her chin, hugged her knees and glared.

'You'd better explain.'

'It's easy.' Nate gestured around them at the magnificent bedroom. 'This place is huge. We have six bedrooms. The doctor who built this was into palaces. He went bankrupt, by the way—but that was forty years ago so let's not worry about him.'

'Oh, right. Let's not.'

'But he left us this great place, and we've modernised it really well. The hospital's a wonderful little set-up and the house is magnificent. We have a garden with huge trees—you can see them from here. They're full of hiding places and are great for climbing. Graham brought his kids up here so the place is kid-proof and there are cubby houses and tree houses and swings and…'

'Stop!'

But he wasn't stopping. 'Mrs McCurdle—our house-keeper—"does" for us, and she loves kids.'

'What on earth…?'

'And we're desperate for another doctor.'

And there it was. Stunning in its simplicity.

We're desperate for another doctor.

The words swam round and round Gemma's head, like some crazy rhyme she couldn't decipher the meaning of.

'London Bridge is falling down…falling down…falling down…'

The nursery rhyme suddenly sounded really appropriate. Her sense of order was crumbling around her.

'I'm an anaesthetist,' she said at last, faintly, and he grinned.

'Perfect.' He beamed. 'I'm a surgeon so it's perfect.'

A surgeon. 'You're kidding.'

'Would I kid about something as important as that? I'm actually Mr Ethan but that just confuses the locals. They want a family doctor so a family doctor they have. But I'm a fully paid-up member of the Australian College of

Surgeons, so if you've an appendix you'd like to be rid of then call on me. I'm your man.'

Was Nate always laughing? He stood smiling down at her and it was all she could do not to throw something at him.

'Will you be serious?'

And all of a sudden he was. 'I'm deadly serious,' he told her. 'This place is screaming for another doctor. We're desperate. Graham can't do anaesthetics any more, so all our surgery has to go to the city. I'm run off my legs. I have no social life to speak of—'

'Except for Donna.' It was a stupid thing to say but she couldn't help herself.

'Donna fits in at the edges.'

'Poor Donna.' She glared at him. 'This job offer... It wouldn't have anything to do with the fact that as of yesterday you have a daughter, would it?'

'No, I—'

'You think you'll ask me to stay so that I can take care of Mia?'

'No.' His voice firmed on that one. And then that lurking twinkle appeared behind his eyes—as if he couldn't help himself. 'Though if you're offering...'

'No. I'm not offering. Do you intend to keep her in hospital for ever?'

'I'll take steps...'

'What steps? You'll marry Donna?'

'I haven't made up my mind about that,' he said with a wounded dignity that still contained a trace of lurking laughter. 'I'm working on it.'

'By asking me to stay?'

'No.' And he was serious then. 'No. I spent a large part of last night awake...'

'As you would when you've just found out you're a father.'

He ignored her. 'And I thought about you.'

'Me?'

'You need to look after yourself.'

'And I'll do it by becoming a country doctor?'

'There are worse fates. It'd give Cady the childhood he's missing out on now.'

'He's not missing out…'

'Gemma, face facts. He's a little boy with special needs. More special now that he's a diabetic. He's lost his mum, as far as I know he doesn't have a dad—all he has is you and you're spending your life making enough money to support him. But if you moved here… Gemma, you could cut back your hours. Cady would be just through the door while you worked. Every time you stopped for a cup of coffee he'd be here. Mrs McCurdle would love him to bits—and he wouldn't need to be separated from his baby sister.'

She glared even harder at that, latching onto his last point like a terrier to a bone. 'I might have known we'd get back to Mia.'

'She is Cady's half-sister,' he said gently. 'You need to face it.'

'But…' She shook her head, trying to clear the gathering fog. 'I don't want to be a country doctor.'

'Don't you? Have you ever thought about it?'

'No. I—'

'You know, it's not such a bad life. I came down for a few weeks to help Graham out—that was six years ago and I'm still here.'

'I don't—'

'You don't know.' Nate smiled, his all-enveloping smile that had her heart doing things it had no business doing. 'Tell you what. Why don't you get yourself dressed, come out and join us for breakfast and then I'll take you on a tour? We'll go from there. One step at a time, Dr Campbell. What about it?'

And he smiled again and walked out of the room.

Join us for breakfast...

Join who?

Gemma had a long shower and tried to make her muddled mind process her overload of problems.

She'd lost her job. But, facing facts, with Margot's attitude that had been inevitable, and if Nate's lawyer friend could win her compensation that would be nothing but relief for the time being.

She'd have to work somewhere.

Alan?

Leave Alan out of it, she told herself harshly. He hadn't been near since Fiona's death and, please, God, he'd stay away.

He'd know by now that she'd quit. He knew everything...

Ignore Alan!

She'd have to move. So why not move here?

Cady would love it.

Her heart twisted when she thought of her little boy. He'd had it so tough. He'd had a couple of years of living with Fiona—and Alan—where he'd had nothing but neglect. And then he'd come to live with her and...

Damn, she should have noticed the diabetes. Had medicine taught her nothing?

She closed her eyes, going over and over the last few weeks. In hindsight the diagnosis was so obvious.

He'd love it here. This was a great place for him to regain his health.

Could she work here?

Join us for breakfast. Nate's throw-away line played in her head. Again and again.

Join who? Nate and Donna?

She couldn't live here with the pair of them. The idea was ridiculous. And how would it fit with Mia?

She'd be an unpaid nanny, she thought, because if Nate and his precious Donna didn't love Mia to bits then she'd be forced to step in and take her back. She knew she would.

She'd tried hard not to admit it to herself but she knew the truth. Despite her resentment at the hand fate had played her, she loved the baby already.

Damn. Damn, damn and damn. She towel-dried her hair with a viciousness that brought tears to her eyes. How dared they put her in this situation? Fiona and Nate and Donna. How could they ask the impossible?

She tugged on her jeans and T-shirt. Heck, they were already travel-stained but she had nothing else to wear. She pulled back her curls into the same frayed ribbon and turned to face the mirror.

Her reflection stared back. She was big-eyed and her eyes were still shadowed with fatigue. And grief. Still there from Fiona's death. There'd been so little time for grieving. She was waif-thin. Her jeans were at least a size too big and her T-shirt could be any size at all.

'Why on earth is he offering you a job?' she asked her reflection. 'You're hardly desirable.

'He doesn't want anyone desirable. He wants a medical degree and a mothercraft nurse. You're perfect. He wants to offload his baby.

'Well, he's not offloading her onto me. No way.'

She slammed down the hairbrush and shoved her feet into her sneakers—and then took off to breakfast. To find the mysterious 'us'.

CHAPTER FOUR

'Us' DIDN'T include Donna. Us was Nate, a white-haired gentleman who looked like he was nearing eighty and one pink crib complete with baby.

Gemma walked in the kitchen door and stopped short. She wasn't sure what shocked her most—the sight of Nate with his baby by his side or the sight of the kitchen.

It was an amazing kitchen.

It matched her bedroom, she thought, stunned by its size alone. It was the kitchen of a great house.

The fireplace took up almost a whole wall and looked as if once it had been an open fire complete with spits. The irons were still set in the wall, but now a vast old Aga took up a quarter of the fireplace, and a modern range stood beside it.

The elderly man was making toast. Tall, thin and weathered with age, his white hair held just a trace of the same burnt red as Nate's. He was casually dressed in a soft cashmere pullover and worn carpet slippers. The fire door of the stove was open and he was holding a toasting fork to the flames.

He looked a lot like Nate...

She was trying hard not to look at Nate until she had her bearings.

What else? The table was in proportion to the kitchen—huge. It was scrubbed oak and big enough to seat a dozen with room to spare. There were four squashy armchairs and a settee to match. A faded rug was thrown over a worn, cobbled floor. On the edge of the rug an ancient collie was dozing in front of the fire. Past them all were big doors with inset windows, leading to a wide veranda. From there a path meandered through the garden to the river beyond.

It looked…wonderful.

And Nate? Finally she let herself focus on Nate. He was slicing bread, supervising everything. The crib was beside him, and Mia was fast asleep.

The sight was so unexpected that it rendered her speechless. The whole scene was unbelievably good.

As she paused in the doorway all eyes swung to her— well, the old man's, Nate's and the dog's anyhow. As far as Gemma could see, Mia wasn't the least bit interested, but she was the only one who wasn't inspecting her from the toes up, making her blush with their blatant assessment.

Nate was the first to speak.

'Good morning, sleepyhead. Toast?' Inspection over, he greeted her with his devastating smile—and she had to pinch herself to make sure she wasn't dreaming. Compared to the spartan hospital apartment she was used to, this was heaven.

Then the old man spoke, in a voice that was a husky echo of Nate's. 'I'd accept if I were you,' he advised her. His smile matched Nate's, intensifying her impression that these two were related. 'It's good.' He flipped two pieces of golden toast onto the plate beside him. 'Toasting is the skill I'm most proud of. After fishing and medicine.' He smiled again and the likeness to Nate was even greater. They *had* to be kin. 'You must be Gemma. Dr Campbell. Pardon me if I don't get up but this toasting is a very serious business.'

It hurt him to rise. Gemma could see that. There were two walking sticks propped against the old man's chair which told their own story.

'Don't let me disturb you,' she said quickly. 'And, yes, I'd love some toast.' She cast an uncertain glance at Nate and then she let herself look at the baby. Nate's baby. 'You've brought Mia in here.'

'Very observant.' Nate smiled again, a smile that had the capacity to knock her sideways. His smile was teasing—enticing—heart-warming. 'There were rumours of Golden Staph finding its way quick smart from Sydney so we whisked her out of harm's way.'

He was laughing at her. The rat. 'You didn't need to.'

'No.' His smile faded. 'I didn't need to.' He looked at her for a long minute, taking in the stained clothes and the weariness still on her face. 'I shouldn't have woken you. You should have slept longer.'

'I couldn't.'

'No.' He hesitated, as if wanting to say more, but finally decided against it. 'Gemma, this is Graham Ethan—my Uncle Graham. Graham, meet Gemma. Dr Campbell. Oh, and this is Rufus, the dog, but he won't rise for an introduction. Not unless there's toast involved.'

Graham would have risen then but Gemma was next to him, taking the old man's hand before he could move. 'I'm really pleased to meet you.'

'I'm pleased to meet you, too.' Graham's old eyes examined her face and found what he was searching for. 'You're not like your sister.' It wasn't a question. It was a statement of fact.

'No.' Gemma's chin tilted a little at that. She wasn't. 'My sister was beautiful.'

'Beauty is in the eye of the beholder,' he said ambiguously. 'But you *are* a doctor?'

'Yes.'

'And you've landed a daughter on our Nathan.'

'I didn't land a baby on your Nathan,' she said dryly. 'Dr Ethan landed a baby on himself. I had absolutely nothing to do with it.'

'And you don't want anything to do with her now?'

'No.' But she cast an uncertain glance at the crib and the old doctor's eyes caught her glance and understood. He nodded but had the sense to move on.

'Nate says you want to work here.'

Her glance was to Nate this time. 'I don't see that Nate's giving me a choice but I need to think about it first.'

'You're an anaesthetist?'

'Yes.'

'Why are you an anaesthetist?' Nate asked her. He pulled a chair out for her and waited until she sat. The feeling of being railroaded intensified. She was being seated and breakfasted whether she wanted it or not.

That was ridiculous. Of course she wanted breakfast.

'Um...'

'Get yourself around this toast first,' the old doctor said. 'Nate, leave the girl alone. Make her some eggs and bacon. She looks like she hasn't had a decent meal for months.'

'After Tony's effort last night...'

'One meal does not a banquet make.' Graham snorted. 'Bacon, Nate. Now.'

'Yes, sir.' Nate grinned and started cooking.

But the question returned. *Why are you an anaesthetist?*

She let herself think about it while she ate, aware that they were courteously letting her be to enjoy her breakfast. Yet the question still hung.

Why was she an anaesthetist?

Because of Alan?

The pressure from Alan was something she couldn't explain in a million years, she thought, and it wasn't something they'd want to know. They were simply checking her out—making sure of her. They really wanted another doctor, but not if she'd turn out to be a disaster like Fiona.

At least she could reassure them about that.

'If you're asking whether I'm dependable, I am,' she

told them, and they nodded in unison. They really were very alike.

'Nate told me that,' Graham said, and Gemma cast Nate a startled glance. What else had he told Graham?

'Whatever he's said, I don't want to stay here.' But her tone was unsure.

'Why are you an anaesthetist?' Nate asked again, and she paused, bit into her toast and forced herself to stop panicking—stop feeling like she was being unduly pressured—and think.

'I'm good at it.'

'Is that the only reason?'

'No.'

'Well?'

Leaving Alan out of it—why else? Why?

'I...I run a pain clinic,' she said hesitantly. 'At Sydney Central. It seemed an important thing to do.' And it was true. The pain clinic gave her an enormous amount of satisfaction. Maybe not as much as family medicine could, but it kept Alan happy. Or...maybe happy was too strong a word. It kept him off her back.

And it was a response that pleased the two men questioning her. 'I knew it.' Nate's voice rose on a note of triumph. 'Didn't I tell you?' he demanded of Graham. He turned back to Gemma. 'So you didn't go into anaesthetics to make money?'

Anger surged—because his question had just enough truth in it to sting. But she wasn't admitting that. 'Why should you think I'm in it for the money? I'm good at what I do—and I enjoy it.'

'I'll bet you are.'

'And I've always been interested in pain relief.' She hesitated but then continued. 'My grandpa... He died of bone metastases and his pain control was less than perfect. I thought...well, after he died I had to make a choice about

specialising and I thought maybe I could make a difference.' And as soon as she'd decided on anaesthetics there
had been Alan—and no possibility of backing out.

But Nate had moved on. 'We could set up a pain clinic
here.' His tone was triumphant. 'Gemma, this district…we
feed to Blairglen but the district itself is huge. If you were
to set up a pain clinic here you'd have half a practice
without even advertising. If you're prepared to do home
visits the local hospice nurses would fall on your neck.'

'But I don't want—'

'Don't want what? Do you really like living in the city?'
he demanded, and his question almost took her breath
away.

Did she like the city? She'd never thought about it.

She'd been raised in Sydney's inner suburbs. By the
time she'd had a choice about leaving, her grandfather had
been ill and depending on her. And then there had been
Fiona… And Alan. And Cady.

'You've never given it a shot.' Nate's tone was still
exultant. 'Hell, Gemma, you can do as much good here as
in the city. More. A competent anaesthetist who's interested in pain relief… You can't leave. You can't.'

'She can,' Graham said dryly without raising his voice.
'Leave the girl be, Nate. You're pushing too hard.'

'I'm not.'

'You are. Make Gemma some coffee.'

'But—'

'Slow down, Nate.' The doctor's old eyes were warm
and understanding. 'Gemma, don't look like that. Like
we're holding you prisoner and throwing away the key.
We're not.'

'But—'

'But we're asking you to give us a chance.' His smile
was exactly the same as his nephew's. Magnetic in its

warmth. 'Give this place a try. Nate says you're without a job and your little nephew needs a chance to recover.'

'He needs the city,' she said, distressed. 'A paediatrician...'

'If you'll trust us then we can help there,' the old doctor said gently, and she frowned.

'You?'

'I may be seventy-six but I'm not useless and neither is Nate.' He saw her uncertainty and went on without giving her a chance to voice her doubts. 'I'm a diabetic myself and I have been for fifty years. There's nothing like suffering a complaint yourself for focusing the mind on current research—and as my health has deteriorated Nate's knowledge has grown. There's not a lot about current diabetic practice that Nate doesn't know, and we have friends who specialise in paediatric diabetes who are on the end of the phone. We know enough to call them when we need them.'

Gemma didn't know what to say. She didn't want to hurt their feelings but...

'We'll have Jacob Burt call you,' Nate told her.

'Jacob...' She knew Jacob. He was one of Sydney Central's leading paediatricians and she knew he was an internationally acknowledged leader in paediatric diabetic management. It was Jacob she'd been thinking of when she'd said she had to get Cady back to Sydney.

'Graham's travelled up to Sydney once a fortnight for thirty years and now I've taken over,' Nate told her, seeing her doubts. 'We've been part of Jacob's research team. It's been damnably difficult with Graham ill—finding the time—but it's the one link with the outside medical world we've fought to retain. But you don't need to take our word for it. I rang Jacob last night to check that I was doing the right thing, and if you like I'll have Jacob call you to confirm it.'

This was the truth. She met Nate's look and she knew without a doubt that Jacob would confirm every word that she'd just heard.

There were diabetic experts right here. That meant that for a short while—just while she got her bearings, or at least until Alan interfered—she could stay here.

She could be a part of this.

She looked around her—at the two men watching her with grave courtesy. At the baby sleeping steadily in her crib. At the flickering firelight and the snoozing dog.

They were asking her to be part of it.

As Fiona had been.

Fiona had been a fool.

'Stay for a couple of weeks,' Nate said softly. 'Give us a trial.'

Damn, he was smiling that smile again. The smile that had had Fiona deciding she wanted his baby. The smile that could break a woman's heart just by—

No! She wasn't going down that road. She had more sense.

She could try it out. Just for two weeks. Alan would surely grant her that. And then she could walk away.

They were both watching her. Waiting.

And suddenly it was easy.

'For a couple of weeks? Yes, please,' she said, and as she smiled back at the pair of them she thought, What on earth have I done?

Graham left them soon after.

'There's a spot of fishing calling,' he told them, and smiled. 'As long as you don't need me?'

'We don't need you,' Nate said and as the old man left, the ancient dog at his heels, Nate smiled at Gemma like a conspirator.

'You don't know how good it is to tell him that,' he

told her. 'Just knowing he doesn't have to carry his mobile phone, he'll be able to spend the morning on the river with the knowledge that if there's an emergency I have you. I won't have to call him back.'

So they were depending on her already. It felt…strange. Like fine gossamer threads of netting were gently settling on her shoulders. Holding her whether she willed it or not.

And then Mrs McCurdle, the woman who 'did' for them, bustled into the kitchen. She enveloped Mia in her overpowering maternal bosom. Nate gave Gemma a sideways grin and ushered her out, giving her the sensation that they were making their escape. Maybe it wasn't just Gemma who felt like she was being trapped. Mrs McCurdle, burbling on about the doctor's new wee baby, obviously made Nate feel exactly the same.

'She's a good soul,' Nate told her as they made their way through to the hospital. 'But a little bit of her goes a long way.'

'I can see that.'

But his thoughts had moved onto medicine. 'Let's see to your nephew. To Cady.'

She didn't have to ring Jacob. Nate was every bit as good as his word. Not only did he have the skills but he also had the technology to back him up.

Cady was just waking when they reached him but he wasn't the least bit scared. The experience of the crèche had left him unafraid of new people, and Nate had a team of skilful and kindly nurses who were just great with Cady.

Nate was great himself. He wheeled the equipment he needed into the ward and set about testing Cady's blood-sugar level, explaining what he was doing to Cady every step of the way. So much so that Cady hardly noticed the pinprick on his finger as Nate took blood. Nate had him press the buttons on the machine and he was so interested in the technology he didn't even think of being frightened.

And they had what they needed within minutes. 'His sugar levels have been high for at least three months,' Nate told Gemma, showing her the readout. 'Look. The build-up on his blood cells is running over nine.'

And she hadn't noticed...

'It's hard to notice changes when you see them every day.' Nate looked at her face and guessed at once what she was feeling. 'You're not to blame yourself.'

'How can I help it? If I'd seen—'

'There's no long-term damage done. We have his sugar down to twelve already.' He looked at Cady who was studying the slip of test paper that held his blood and looking at the screen showing his results. His bright little face said he was already trying to figure out how things worked. 'It's my guess that he'll be giving himself injections and testing himself in no time.'

'He's only four.'

But Nate was still watching Cady and he shook his head. 'Maybe he is only four but this is Cady's medical condition, Gemma,' he said gently. 'His. And the sooner he owns it the better. If you take responsibility for it then Cady doesn't need to and there'll be rebellion in the future. Sure, he's small, but just as soon as he can conquer a skill—like giving himself an injection or deciding that a food's bad for him—then you let him do the deciding. It's the only way for him to cope with his future. To feel like he's in control.'

Gemma thought back to her sister. To the dreadful fights between mother and daughter from the moment of Fiona's diagnosis, over and over again. The shouting matches. 'You can't eat that,' her mother had decreed, terrified at what had been happening to her favourite daughter. 'What's your blood sugar?'

Fiona had loathed it, nearly always eating exactly what she shouldn't have.

Maybe if she'd been treated differently…

Who could tell? All that Gemma knew was that Nate's gentle words made sense. For now she'd go with him.

'Fine.'

'Now, let's work on an insulin regime,' Nate told her, moving right on. 'Cady's growing stronger by the minute.' The night on the saline drip had worked wonders.

'You think he'll be fine?'

'I'm sure he'll be fine. Why wouldn't he be?'

Cady might be improving but he was still a very tired little boy. He was awake for barely half an hour before his eyes were closing again and Gemma tucked him back into bed. Which left her free.

But Nate wasn't free. Out the hospital window she could see people arriving at the clinic to see him. He had a full day's consulting before him.

'Let me help,' she urged.

He shook his head. 'Not today.'

'I can.'

'I'm very sure you can.' His tone was gentle—full of caring—and it had the capacity to unsettle her in a way she didn't fully understand. 'But you're still suffering from the shock of last night and I don't want you. Tomorrow I'll set you to work but today is declared a Gemma-holiday.'

A Gemma-holiday. She'd never heard of such a thing. There had been so much on her shoulders lately she hadn't known which way to turn. And sleep… She'd slept more last night than she'd slept for a month and here was this man urging her to have more.

'I don't need—'

'You do need.' Nate took her shoulders and propelled her to the glass doors opening onto the veranda. 'There's

a hammock down by the river which is my very favourite
spot in the whole world. Go find it, Dr Campbell. And use
it.'

'But—'

'No buts. You get yourself rested and recovered. Now.'
He gave her a gentle push toward the edge of the veranda—and then walked inside and closed the door firmly
behind her.

She was free to wander as she willed.

The sensation was so novel Gemma could hardly take
it in. How long had it been since she'd had some time to
herself? Years.

Dazed, she wandered down to the river, and there was
Nate's hammock. It was slung between two trees right at
the water's edge. The sun was dappling through the leaves
of the huge eucalypts and the water was rippling between
boulders, making a lullaby all by itself. The setting was
just perfect. She could see why it was Nate's favourite
place.

She could see Nate here.

But he wasn't here. He was working. As she should be
working. She always worked.

But what had Nate said? *It's a Gemma-holiday.*

'I shouldn't,' she told herself. But she did. The sun was
warm on her face, the river was rippling and gurgling,
there were kookaburras chortling in the gums overhead…

Cady was sleeping. Cady was recovering. Mia was being well cared for by the redoubtable Mrs McCurdle.

God was in his heaven. All was right with her world.
For now.

She climbed into the hammock and looked up through
the eucalypts at the sky above. And slept.

'Will it be my lot in life, ad infinitum, to wake you up?'

She opened her eyes. Nate's face was six inches away

from hers and he was laughing at her. 'Hey, sleepyhead, it's almost dinnertime.'

Dinnertime.

Dinnertime! She sat up with such a jolt that the hammock veered crazily sideways. She would have fallen but Nate reached out and caught her shoulders, steadying her. And when she was steady he didn't pull his hands away.

'Are you OK?'

Was she OK? She thought about it. She was warm and sleepy and incredibly comfortable—and Nate was holding her as if he cared. Was she OK? Yes. A whole lot more than OK.

'I'm fine.' She pulled back a little but he didn't release her.

'We were starting to get worried.'

'Worried?' She sounded dazed. It was the feel of his hands, she thought. It made her feel...well, dazed.

'I checked at lunchtime and found you sleeping, but I couldn't believe you'd keep sleeping this long. If your car wasn't still parked outside I would have thought you'd bolted back to Sydney.'

She looked at him, astonished. 'Are you kidding? How could I have left Cady?'

'No.' His eyes were still inches from hers. Questioning her with no need for words. 'No, I guess you wouldn't do that.'

'I wouldn't.'

Nate's gaze was still probing. 'And yet you'd leave Mia?'

'Mia is your baby. Not mine.' She pulled away from him then and sat up. The hammock swung wildly again and she had to shove her feet down fast to hold herself steady. She missed his hands. They were good hands, she thought inconsequentially. Big. Warm and strong and capable. Doctor's hands.

She was being ridiculous.

And he was watching her as if he could read her mind.

'I shouldn't have gone to sleep,' she said quickly—too quickly—and he smiled, with the indulgence of an adult giving a child a treat.

'Of course you should. Your nephew has slept the day away and I've a feeling his aunt needed the sleep even more. If Cady hadn't collapsed I think you would have collapsed in his stead. How long have you been burning the candle at both ends?'

She thought about it. 'I guess... There has been so much to do. Since Fiona died. And Mia isn't a restful baby—as you'll no doubt find out.'

'She looks pretty restful to me.'

'Yeah. And how long have you stayed with her?'

'Hours and hours.' He gave her a look of pure unsullied virtue which made her smile.

'Yeah, right.'

But he was moving on. 'Do you want a hospital tour before dinner? We have time.'

'Um...'. She looked down at her rumpled self. 'I guess. Though I'm not exactly looking my professional best.'

'You look pretty good to me.'

There it was again. That jolt. It was a stab of warmth that had her understanding exactly why Fiona had chosen him to be the father of her child.

'Yeah, right.' She didn't meet his eyes—just scuffed her trainers on the grass and looked up toward the hospital. 'OK. Lead the way.' He looked every inch the doctor and she looked every inch the poor relation.

So what else was new?

Fiona had made her feel like an also-ran from the moment of her birth. She should be used to it by now.

'It's a casual sort of hospital,' he told her, and there it was again—the reading of minds that she was starting to dread. 'No specialists with bow-ties need apply. The people here are farmers and they don't look for sophistication. They look for caring—and it seems to me that caring's what you have in spades.'

Of course. Caring was what she was principally good at.

Caring...

It went on and on for ever.

Once on her tour of inspection, however, Gemma forgot her concerns about her appearance. She forgot everything except the hospital, and the hospital was great.

The doctor who'd built it all those years ago had suffered delusions of grandeur and had built a hospital that could have accommodated three times the number of beds they had.

'We're accredited for twenty patients,' Nate told her as she exclaimed at the size of the place. 'And no one can say we're crowded.'

They certainly weren't. The wards were double or single and they were roomy, comfortably furnished and ever so slightly over the top.

'There were chandeliers here when my uncle arrived,' Nate told her. 'He got rid of them because of the dust— and because the local farmers thought they'd died and gone to heaven. They'd have a minor operation and wake up to this—and damn near arrest on the spot.'

'I can imagine.' Gemma looked up at the high pressed ceilings with their ornate cornices and beautifully moulded plasterwork and shook her head in disbelief. 'All you need is a few Michelangelo friezes and you could be in the Sistine Chapel.'

'Maybe we could have a working bee and paint a few.'

Nate was grinning down at her. Life was a constant joke to him, Gemma thought with just a trace of anger. Then his smile caught her and she had to smile back. Sort of.

'A working bee to paint the ceilings...' She smiled. 'What a great idea. Can I help? I paint a really mean elephant. From the rear.'

'I'll bet you do.'

And they were grinning at each other like fools and it took Mrs Draper—an elderly lady with gout—harrumphing from her bed to haul them back to order.

Over the top or not, the hospital was run as a well-oiled machine. The staff greeted Gemma with interest, chatting to Nate with real friendliness. There was nothing of the distance between nurses and doctors she saw in the big city hospitals.

And the patients were the same. Nate greeted them with ease and introduced them to Gemma in turn. They chatted, they checked Gemma out with a curiosity she saw would instantly turn to gossip the moment they left, and in the end she was left feeling as if the place consisted of one big family.

'That's what country practice is all about,' Nate told her as she exclaimed over the sensation. 'Do you want to give us a go?'

And at the end of the tour she felt her doubts dissipating. This could work. It could.

'Yes, please.'

'That's great.' His smile was so intimate it warmed parts of her she hadn't begun to realise were cold.

'Fantastic,' he told her. 'Let's go to dinner.'

Dinner was lovely. Sitting in the huge kitchen, listening to Graham and Nate gossip over the events of the day, Gemma felt more and more at home. Mrs McCurdle had left them the king of all casseroles. Mia was gurgling sleepily in her cot, the dog was asleep again before the fire and it felt like family. And family was something Gemma hadn't felt for a very long time.

'Gemma?'

Nate was talking to her, she realised, and she had to blink to haul herself back to reality. She'd been floating in a fuzzy little dream where country practice, Cady and Mia—and Nate—were all mixed up in a rosy future.

She looked at him blankly. 'Sorry?'

'Penny for your thoughts.'

She blinked at that. 'You don't want to hear them.'

'I bet I do.'

She smiled but she shook her head. 'No way.' If he couldn't guess, she wasn't telling him. 'Was there something you wanted?'

He hesitated and she could see what he was thinking that maybe now wasn't the time to ask. He wanted a favour, she decided, and he was wondering whether she was up to it.

But she'd slept all day and she felt terrific.

'Go on. Ask. I can always refuse.'

His brows rose at that and she thought, Great—he's not the only one who can read minds. Put that in your pipe and smoke it, Nate Ethan.

She'd disconcerted him and it showed. When he spoke again his voice had lost some of its certainty. 'I was wondering…'

'You were wondering what?'

And out it came. 'OK. I was wondering whether you'd cover me tonight.'

She thought about it. 'Medically?'

'Certainly medically.' He smiled that endearing smile that would obtain anything he wanted. 'Graham's involved with the local repertory society—he's playing the Major-

General in their production of *The Pirates of Penzance* and it's their dress rehearsal tonight.'

'The Major-General?' Gemma twinkled across the table at Graham. How wonderful. She could really see him in the role, waving his walking sticks at the pirates and the world in general and thumbing his nose at his disabilities. 'That's fantastic.' She turned back to Nate. 'So don't tell me. You need to go, too, because you're the Pirate King.'

'No.'

Her nose wrinkled in disappointment. 'That's a pity.' She had a great vision of him bare-chested and piratical, complete with cutlass and sword. The thought was enough to make her blink. 'You'd make a wonderful pirate.'

He didn't know how to take that one. 'Thanks very much.'

'Think nothing of it,' she said expansively. The food, the warmth and the overall sense of security were getting to her, making her feel fantastic. 'But if you're not the pirate...'

'I'm not in the play.'

'Oh?'

'Both of us can't be,' he said—as if she was a bit simple not to have thought it through. 'Until now Graham and I haven't been able to go out together. There's always been the need to cover.'

'But now?'

'Now there's you.'

Right. She was here. And she might as well work. Why not? 'And you want to go out?'

'If I can.' There was a knock on the door. 'Whoops. There's Donna now.'

Donna. Right. Donna-the-girlfriend.

'Donna and I were supposed to spend yesterday evening at the Jazzfest,' Nate told her. 'She was a bit upset when I was called away.'

'I imagine she was.' She tried not to mind. Why should she mind? Donna and Nate were nothing to her.

Were they?

'Anyway, there's a party on tonight for a couple of our friends who are getting married this weekend.' He glanced at his watch. 'Starting about now.'

He hadn't gone to answer the door and there was no need. Donna had let herself in. She stood in the doorway looking fabulous in a beige silk pantsuit that must have set her back half a year's salary. She looked gorgeous!

And Gemma felt just like she always did when someone like this was around. Someone like Donna. Someone like Fiona. She felt frumpy and frazzled and like she was middle-aged already. At the ripe old age of twenty-eight.

'Are you ready, love? Have you asked her?' Donna didn't bother to greet either Graham or Gemma, and Graham shoved his plate away with unnecessary force. As if he was suddenly faced with something distasteful.

'If you'll excuse me, I need to be going. I'll be home at about eleven, Gemma.'

Which left Nate and Donna and Gemma. And one sleeping baby.

'You don't mind, do you?' Nate asked politely. 'There shouldn't be any problems. We've gone through every patient's history so there shouldn't be any surprises, but if you're worried give me a call.' He motioned to his cellphone. 'I wear my phone on my belt.'

'I don't mind.' She was trying hard not to.

'That's great.' Donna held out her hand to Nate and he rose and took it. 'Lovely. Let's go, sweetheart, before she changes her mind.'

She... She, the cat's mother?

Gemma told herself she shouldn't mind the way Donna was referring to her. Being a doormat was her role in life. But there was something stirring—the same thing that had stirred when the doctors had placed the newborn Mia in her arms. There was love and commitment—but there was also anger and resolution, and that resolution had to be brought to the fore right now.

'You've forgotten something,' she said flatly as they headed out the door.

'Sorry?' Nate turned, expecting her to point to the car keys or something trivial. 'What?'

'Your daughter.'

'My…' He stared at the crib. 'Mia.'

'That's right.'

'But you can look after her.' It was a statement—not a question—and her anger built.

'I told you, Nate. I won't.'

'But—'

'But last night the hospital staff looked after her and today Mrs McCurdle looked after her. And tonight I'm not. I told you, Nate—she's your daughter. Not mine.'

CHAPTER FIVE

'YOU have to be kidding.' Donna was staring at her as if she'd lost her mind.

'Why should I be kidding?' Gemma's tone was flat and lifeless, which was exactly how she felt. Nate was using her. Of course. Why on earth had she expected anything else?

'Gemma, she'll probably sleep,' Nate told her, reasonableness personified. 'And you're going to be here anyway.'

'I want to go and sit by Cady.'

'Cady will be asleep. But, of course, you can go into the hospital. Mia will be only through the door and if there are any problems with patients you can wheel her through to kids' ward.'

She glowered. 'I might want to go for a walk.'

'Then wheel her through to the hospital and take your phone. The staff will call you if she wakes.'

'No.'

'No?'

She stood and faced them. OK. She was about to be a totally unreasonable human being but it had to be done. She could see her time here stretching into the future. Doctor, Cady's mother and Mia's mum by default.

'I told you, Nate—'

'Gemma, you're being irrational.'

'No. I'm not. I'm keeping myself sane. I told you—I can't afford to get any more attached to Mia. She's your daughter, Nate. If you want to go out then you take her with you.'

'I'm not taking any baby anywhere,' Donna said flatly.

'It's cold outside.' Nate was struggling to be reasonable. 'She'll catch a chill.'

Gemma looked at him in disbelief. 'Oh, how medically sound is that? Catch a chill... What's going to happen? Are all those little bugs labelled ''chill virus'' just hovering round in the night air waiting to strike? That's nonsense, Nate Ethan, and you know it.'

He backed off a bit but persisted. 'She could get cold.'

'Yeah. Leave her naked in the night air and she'll catch hypothermia. Bundle her up in her baby capsule with only her nose poking out, take a change of nappy and a couple of bottles, and she won't know the difference from staying here all night.'

He glowered, and she glowered right back. Force meeting force. 'Gemma, it would be much easier to leave her here, and you know it.'

'Easier for who?'

'For me,' he said, and he suddenly stopped glowering and grinned.

Damn, he just had to smile at her. The great Labradorpuppyish grin had the capacity to take her breath away. That was the way he always got what he wanted, she decided—but he wasn't getting it now.

Fiona had wheedled what she'd wanted by smiling just like that. Fiona and Nate... They were a pair in more ways than one, and she wanted nothing to do with it. She was through with being manipulated.

'No,' she said flatly, and backed against the sink. She was holding her empty plate before her like a shield, as if he was likely to broach her defence by sheer emotional force. Which was entirely possible.

'Gemma...'

'No!'

'You really mean it?'

'I really mean it. If you go out then you take your daughter with you.'

Accepting finally the impossibility of working on Gemma, Nate turned to Donna.

'I'm not—' Donna started.

'Love…'

'No.'

'If we don't take her I'll have to stay home.'

Donna hesitated. She really wanted Nate, Gemma could see. But she didn't want attachments. Well, why should she? Gemma asked herself, thinking of Cady sleeping peacefully just the other side of the wall. She knew more than most that attachments hurt.

'If we take her tonight then you'll want to take her everywhere,' Donna was saying. 'She's not going to change her mind.'

At least Donna understood, Gemma decided. At least Donna could see it.

'Just for tonight…'

'No.' Donna's voice was suddenly just like Gemma's. Implacable. 'Kids don't interest me, Nate. Hell, we'd be stuck. I mean, having a kid in the back seat…'

It would cramp her style, Gemma thought, not without sympathy. But her twinge of sympathy wasn't enough to let her relent.

'Gemma…' Nate had turned to her again.

'No!'

'Hell!' Nate closed his eyes. 'Gemma, this is just plain unreasonable.'

'Ring the discrimination board,' she said flatly. 'They'll tell you how reasonable it is to expect a work colleague to look after your children.'

'I don't—'

'You do. That's what this is. Coercion. Do you want me as a doctor or do you want me as a babysitter?'

'As a doctor, of course.'

'Then look after your own kid.'

'We're giving you your keep for nothing...'

That was all she needed! Her eyes flashed fury. 'Then I'll move into the motel tonight.' She slammed the plate into the sink and stalked to the door. 'Thanks for the bed last night. Send me the bill for accommodation when you bill me for Cady's medical expenses.'

'Gemma, don't be ridiculous.'

'Goodbye, Nate,' she said, and walked out the door, slamming it behind her. Before the pair of them could see the tears of frustrated rage welling in her eyes.

'Gemma?'

'Go away. I'll be out of here in five minutes.' She was shoving her hairbrush into her handbag. She had nothing else to pack, she thought bitterly, which made stalking out in style a whole lot easier.

Hopefully the motel would have a vacant room. Otherwise she'd sleep in the car, and as soon as Cady was well enough to travel she'd bundle him up and take him back to Sydney.

The thought was immeasurably bleak and those damned tears threatened to fall.

'Gemma...' The door of her bedroom swung open and Nate was there. Nate with his face wary—as if he expected the hairbrush in her hand to come whizzing across the room at him.

'What?' She was so angry she was almost speechless.

'Gemma, I didn't mean—'

'You did mean.'

Hell!

He stared across at her, baffled in the face of her fury. She had two burning patches of colour on her cheeks, giving life to her otherwise too-pale face, and her eyes were shining. With unshed tears?

Damn, he'd made her cry. All at once he felt like a king-sized rat.

'Gemma, I'm sorry.'

'There's no need to apologise. You're right. I owe you heaps. But I won't pay it off by taking over your responsibilities. By taking on your baby. Just add my board to Cady's bill, charge us for what we owe you and be done with it.'

'We won't be billing for Cady.'

'Of course you will. Why wouldn't you?'

'Because you're a colleague. We don't charge colleagues.'

'Colleagues don't babysit. Unless they offer.'

'You're right,' he said gravely, watching her face.

Would she still walk? He'd messed it up, he thought. Hell, he'd nearly had another doctor for this place and he'd messed it up by pushing too hard, too fast.

But looking at her face…

The void that was threatened was more than the thought of losing a potential partner, he thought, but how much more? He didn't know. He couldn't really figure out what he was feeling right at this minute—except that he didn't want her to go so badly that he'd sent Donna away.

And Donna wouldn't return. She was furious. Babies weren't her scene.

There'd be other Donnas, he thought. Women weren't a problem. He hadn't wanted a long-term relationship with Donna.

He didn't want a long-term relationship with anyone.

But he did want another doctor in this practice. Graham couldn't keep working for much longer and the workload was crazy. Gemma could well be the answer.

Which was why he was standing right here, apologising.

It had nothing to do with the look of blind misery on her face. Nothing at all. It was the sensible, practical thing to do.

As was crossing the room in two strides and taking her shoulders in his hands. Forcing her chin up so her tear-drenched eyes met his.

'I'm sorry.'

'I'm not crying.' She gave a desperate sniff. 'I never cry. I must have hay fever or something.'

'Of course. I can give you some pills for hay fever.' But he felt in his pocket and brought out something that was far more useful. 'Meanwhile, how about a handkerchief?'

'Thank you.' She took it and blew—hard. It was a sound never heard from the likes of Donna or Fiona. It was un-feminine, loud and almost defiant in its misery.

And it touched him as nothing else could.

'Better?' He smiled down at her and she glared back through unshed tears.

'Yes. No. I told you, I have hay fever and hay fever doesn't cure itself with one nose blow.'

'Of course it doesn't. But if I upset you—on top of your hay fever...'

'You have no power to upset me.'

'No. But if I did then I'm sorry.'

'You don't have to be sorry. You're going out, remember. Just take your lady and your baby and go.'

'I'm not going anywhere.'

'Donna won't take the baby?'

Donna certainly wouldn't. 'Um...no.'

'Well, don't expect me to apologise because your love life has been interrupted. It's not my fault. Mia is your daughter and she has nothing to do with me.'

'I know that.'

'So I'm leaving.'

'Gemma, I want you to stay. I really, really want you to stay.'

There was silence while she took that on board. Silence, silence and more silence.

'I don't want...' she started finally, but her voice was unsure and he shook his head. Once more his hands came out to grasp her shoulders. Damn, she was so thin. There was nothing of her. She'd have to stay so Mrs McCurdle could build her up. Make her curvy...

She'd look good curvy.

She looked good now.

'You do want,' he said, his tone gentling. 'You want very much to stay. From your perspective this place has everything going for it—except me. Except a doctor who's ready to face his responsibilities.'

'Yes, but—'

'But if I'm prepared to try then will you give us a try? Will you give me another chance, Gemma?'

She sniffed and tried to glare but it didn't quite come off. 'I'm not looking after Mia.'

'I'm not asking you to.'

'You promise?'

'I promise.'

She stared up into his eyes. She doesn't believe me, Nate thought, and then decided that she had the right to have doubts. He had doubts himself.

'I should go. I'm crazy to stay.'

'No. You're sensible.'

'There's not a single thing sensible about it.'

'You want me to list all the very sensible reasons why you should stay?'

'No.' Gemma backed away from him and her scowl returned. 'You could talk your way out of an iron lung.'

'I bet I couldn't.'

'I bet you could. There's nothing I wouldn't put past you.'

'No.' That was enough. It was time he called a halt. 'Gemma, what have I ever done to you to make you distrust me?'

'You made my sister pregnant.'

But Nate wasn't buying into that one. 'Gemma, if your sister wanted to get pregnant then she was going to get pregnant, whether it was with me or with someone else. You're right in thinking I was a fool to let myself be used, but she'd decided to self-destruct anyway. She used me just as she used you. You've been more deeply hurt than I have but I won't add to that hurt. For what it's worth, you can trust me.'

Now, why had he said that? Why had he suddenly made the conversation so deadly serious?

It was the way she was looking, he thought—as if the bottom had dropped out of her world. And why?

It was because he'd offered her a way out, he thought bitterly. He'd offered her a life here as a country doctor and a future for herself and her nephew—and then he'd hauled it away again with one stupid, senseless act. Assuming she'd look after Mia.

'I won't try to palm the baby off on you again,'

'The baby...' she repeated, and she winced.

He thought it through and heard where she was coming from. Maybe it did sound a bit harsh. *The baby...* He tried again. 'Mia.'

'No.' She fixed him with a look. 'No. She's not "the baby". She's not Mia. She's your daughter. Say it, Nate.'

And he tried. 'My daughter.' Hell. It was harder to say it than he would have thought possible. *My daughter.* It sounded really, really strange.

'Right. Your daughter.'

OK, he'd got over that hurdle. Now the next. 'You wouldn't want to unpack your bag and stay?'

'What? Take my hairbrush out of my handbag?'

'That's the one.' He frowned. She couldn't keep wearing the one pair of jeans for ever. 'We really need to do something about your wardrobe. How about a shopping trip tomorrow?'

'Thanks but I don't need it. I rang a friend in Sydney before I went to sleep this morning. Her apartment's next to mine at Sydney Central. She agreed to gather a few things together and she'll put a suitcase on the train today.'

'Then that's another reason why you can't leave,' he said triumphantly. 'Your clothes will pass you as you speed up the highway—and we'll be stuck here with clothes for a complete doctor but no doctor to put them on.'

'Don't push your luck.'

'No. Right.' He ventured a lopsided grin. He was in complete agreement. A wise man knew when to shut up. 'So now what? I'm not going out and neither are you. How about a game of Scrabble?'

'Scrabble? Instead of a pre-wedding party?'

'I think maybe going to the pre-wedding party was a bad idea.'

She eyed him doubtfully. Did he mean it? 'You know, you could take Mia with you.'

'It wouldn't be the same,' he told her, not without a tinge of regret. 'I'd arrive with the…with my daughter and my nappy bag and my bottle of milk instead of a bottle of wine and Donna would stalk in a hundred yards behind and bad-mouth me for the rest of the evening. And the gossip would be astonishing.'

'So you'd prefer Scrabble?'

'I'm a whizz at Scrabble,' he said modestly—but he didn't look the least bit modest. 'I always win.'

Gemma stared up at him for a long moment and Nate gazed back. There it was again—that lurking twinkle that had the capacity to make her heart do handstands. But…he *was* staying home. He was trying.

Finally she let herself relax. Just a fraction. 'I'm not bad myself.'

'That sounds like a challenge.' His twinkle became a grin. 'And I'm a man who always meets a challenge. So what about it, Dr Campbell? Do you want to play?'

Did she want to play?

Play. It was a word that hadn't been in her vocabulary for a very long time.

But he was smiling down at her and his gorgeous eyes were filled with lurking laughter. And more. They held a hint of caring. She stared up at him. The future of the medical practice of the town hung on this very moment and Nate found he was holding his breath. Would she?

And then, suddenly, she was smiling back at him and it was as if the sun had come out. More. It was a wonderful, wonderful smile.

'OK, Dr Ethan. Bring out your Scrabble board. I'm about to let you know exactly who's boss around here.'

It was a very silly game of Scrabble.

'Piffle!'

'Piffle's a word.' Nate looked wounded to the core that she should suggest otherwise. 'How can you query piffle?'

Informality was definitely the order of the night. They were sprawled on cushions on the rug before the living room fire, Nate had changed into jeans and a sweatshirt that was almost as old as Gemma's, and they might have been playing Scrabble for years. It felt…great, Gemma thought, almost afraid to acknowledge how great it was.

'But if we're speaking of piffle,' Nate said cautiously, eyeing what she was doing with astonishment, 'let's look at this current offering. "Flowery"? Is "flowery" a word?'

'Of course it is. You can say this sofa's all flowery. Or your conversation is flowery.'

'Hey! It is not.'

'It might be.'

'Flowery… Never in a million years.'

'Well, think of Mrs McCurdle talking about her plans for the spring fête… Definitely flowery.'

' "Floury" I might allow, like floury hands when you're making scones.'

'Yeah, but I don't have a U. And if I put "flowery" on the end of your "bull" then "bull" becomes "bully"— which is definitely a word—and "y" is on the double word score. That means I get double scores for both words. With an "o" on a double letter that gives me twenty plus thirty-four—plus a bonus of fifty for using all seven letters. A hundred and four. Wow!' She beamed her satisfaction.

And her beam had him fascinated. She sort of lit up from within.

But there were important issues to concentrate on here. Like winning Scrabble. A man had his pride after all. 'And it's exactly because it's a hundred-and-four-point word that I won't allow it.'

'No?'

'No!'

Gemma let herself look woebegone—cocker-spaniel style. 'Not even because you feel sorry for me?'

'Don't you do the sympathy thing on me. Nothing gets in the way of me and winning a game of Scrabble.'

'Not even brute force?' Laughing, she raised a cushion—and Nate cowered in mock fear.

But then the phone rang. Damn. For some reason it really irritated him, and it wasn't just that he was still in the lead. Reluctantly he rose to answer it while Gemma calmly put down her letters. Flowery… She grinned and added a hundred and four points to her score, which meant she was winning by a mile, but she was listening to what Nate was saying all the while.

And his voice was suddenly serious. 'Right, bring her straight in.'

'Trouble?' she asked as he replaced the receiver. From where she sat he looked big and competent and…nice, she thought. Though it wasn't nice in the sense that Fiona would have thought nice. Fiona would have only seen his body, which was certainly nice enough. Or maybe that was an understatement. But the rest of him—the Nate inside— was pretty darned nice, too.

'I need to go.'

Why did her heart lurch a little? It had been a long time since she'd felt like this, she thought. Warm, contented and full of delicious laughter. He warmed her from the toes up and she hated the thought that her time with him was over. For now.

'What's wrong?'

'An asthmatic. Milly Jefferson. She's five years old and tight as hell. We play a balancing act keeping her at home.'

'Let me help.'

'You don't need to.'

'I want to.' She smiled at him with that smile he was only just getting to know. And like. 'I'm on call tonight and we agreed I'd take over medically while you looked after your baby.'

'But my baby's asleep.' There. He'd said it. My baby. Just like that.

'Then let's go and play doctors,' she said serenely. She pulled herself to her feet and stood waiting. 'Together.'

They did more than play doctors. Their medicine was needed in earnest.

As Nate had said, Milly was as tight as hell. Her parents rushed her into Casualty, their faces desperate with fear.

For good reason. She'd gone past the point where bronchodilators were effective. She'd gone past the point where salbutamol administration was even possible. She lay limp and unresponsive in her father's arms and Gemma took one look and thought, We've lost her.

But Nate was taking her from her parents, laying her on the examination couch and putting the oxygen mask on her face almost in one fluid movement.

Maybe it was too late for the oxygen mask. His fingers were on her pulse. The little girl's chest was still—the fight for breath seemed over.

'I need to intubate...'

Gemma was before him. The nurse on duty hadn't arrived yet—she must have been caught up elsewhere in the hospital—but Gemma had been in the emergency department before when she'd brought Cady in. She knew what was required and where to find it. By the time Nate had checked the child's airway the crash cart was by his side and an intubation tube was being placed in his hand.

There was no time for muscle relaxants—and no need. The child was past the point of fighting.

Nate lifted the tube. Then, on the point of intubation, he paused and motioned to Gemma. 'You.'

She got it in one. She was the anaesthetist. Intubating a child was tricky. Nate might well be able to do this—in fact, he had probably done it many times over his years as a country doctor—but if there was a skilled anaesthetist on hand then why not use her?

So he backed off and prepared an adrenalin injection while Gemma swiftly, expertly slid the tube down the child's throat.

Milly didn't even gag. That was how far she'd gone.

Her mother held her face in her hands, sobbing blindly.

She was buckling at the knees and her husband moved to support her.

But the adrenalin injection slid home and the child's chest heaved in one last convulsive attempt to get air.

Gemma had the bag in place, breathing for her. And the child suddenly found the strength to fight for herself.

Wonderful. The tube was in place. The bag could work, the oxygen could flow and the child could breathe.

She was still that awful colour, though.

'I need muscle relaxant,' Gemma ordered, switching back into doctor mode as if she'd never paused. 'And a sedative. As soon as she recovers she'll fight the tube.'

She looked at Nate. Silently he placed what she needed in her hands and watched as she located a vein in the little girl's hand.

Intravenous drips in children were notoriously difficult but Gemma didn't hesitate. She inserted the drip with no more difficulty than Nate would have experienced had it had been an adult.

'Great.'

And with the drip set up and the child's breathing being supported, they had time to take stock. And breathe themselves.

'She'll make it,' Nate said, and his voice was a trace unsteady. He'd been as scared as she was, Gemma thought, watching him, and then she thought, He cares about his patients. He's not just a womaniser. He's a really fine country practitioner.

And he'd just proved that he wasn't a walking ego either. He'd handed over the intubation to her because he believed her skills were greater than his. It had been a huge vote of confidence in a doctor he didn't know.

'I knew you'd be good,' he said in an undertone, and Gemma felt the colour rise in her face. Compliments like that didn't come her way every day of the week—compliments from the heart.

'Intubation and drips are what I do.'

'You're great.'

'Yeah? As an anaesthetist maybe, but as a country doctor? You say that after I fail to diagnose a case of chickenpox. This is the first time you've seen me work and it's just lucky it was something I'm skilled at.'

'Lucky for Milly...'

'Mmm.'

They stood looking down at the little girl. She was still battling to breathe and she'd need to stay intubated until they were sure her condition was stabilised. Even then there'd be many more of these episodes in her life, Gemma knew—and then she let herself think about Cady. At least diabetes wasn't life-threatening. At least she knew where she was with Cady.

'He'll be fine, too,' Nate said softly, and Gemma raised her head in startled enquiry. What was it with this man? She hated that he could read her mind.

She was a private person. She'd learned the hard way to keep herself to herself and this man's ability to get past the surface had her thoroughly unnerved.

Work. Think about work. Hadn't that always been the best defence? 'We'd best take her though to Children's Ward. Or do you want to keep her in Intensive Care?'

'I have Tom Saunders in Intensive Care with angina so I think we'll take her through to kids' ward. I'll ring for an additional night nurse so we can do one on one while the tube's in.' He looked down at the little girl on the bed and frowned, and his frown wasn't just as a result of complications of the night. He was looking into the future of a child whose condition was increasingly life-threatening. 'This is the fourth acute episode this year. And if we hadn't been close...'

'But you were.'

'I could have been out.'

'And I would have coped.'

He looked at her and he seemed dazed. Like he couldn't quite believe she was real. 'I guess you would have. There are three doctors in this place now. Not two. It's going to take some getting used to.'

'It is.'

'If you stay on…we could do enough surgery to keep you in training, but would you miss doing anaesthetics full time?'

She thought about it.

'Not while there's drama like tonight.' The sedative was starting to take effect now and the child's breathing was becoming relaxed, deeper and more even. She thought, We've just saved her life. It was a good feeling. A great feeling!

As long as they could keep her alive.

'What sort of long-term therapies are you trying?' she asked, and Nate shook his head.

'She's on steroids and bronchodilators as a matter of course. I daren't increase the dosage.'

It was a hard call, Gemma knew. Long-term steroid use had its problems, a major one at this age being that it tended to stunt growth. Milly's parents weren't exactly huge. She'd need every inch of growth she could get.

So move sideways.

'Can Milly swim?'

That caught their attention and suddenly Gemma had them all staring at her. Milly's parents seemed like farmers. They were still dressed for the nightly milking, in stained jeans and work shirts. Their faces were haggard with shock and they held onto each other like they were drowning.

'I… Swim?' Her father was a gruff voiced man in his forties. 'No. Why should she swim? She's only five.'

'It'd be the best thing for her.' She smiled at all of them, Nate included, trying to lessen the tension. 'Exercise builds lung capacity—and swimming's the best form of exercise asthmatics can do.'

'But…she's only five years old.'

'I can teach her.'

'You…' Nate sounded stunned.

'You have an indoor swimming pool,' she said serenely. 'I checked it out this morning when I was exploring and it's wonderful. And I thought what a waste—a swimming pool that's hardly used.'

'I use it.'

'And I imagine Graham does, too. Which means it gets—what? An hour's use a day?'

'Sometimes less,' he conceded, and she grinned.

'Well… That means we have twenty-three hours of available pool time, and me a trained swimming teacher and lifeguard.' She twinkled up at him. 'Teaching swimming was the way I paid my way through university.'

'I see.' But he didn't.

'If I'm here for two weeks I could get Milly started. If we give her a few days to get over the worst of this episode I could give her a week's intensive lessons. I bet I could get her swimming before I leave.' If she left. She was starting to think… Maybe. Maybe this could work.

'You'd really do that?'

'I would.' Gemma's eyes met Nate's, direct and slightly challenging. 'The community here is providing the hospital that takes care of Cady and I intend to put as much into the community as I take out.'

'You'll teach our Milly to swim?' Milly's mother was breathless, clearly finding it hard to take herself away from the drama of the last few minutes and project herself into an unknown future. But she must. A future was what she desperately needed to believe in.

'If it's OK with Dr Ethan.'

'It's more than OK,' Nate declared. 'It's fantastic.'

'Then we have a plan.' Gemma smiled happily at Milly's parents and then she looked back at Nate. 'I'll take Milly through to kids' ward and stay with her until I'm sure she's stable. You ring for the extra nurse and then go back through to the house.'

'But—'

'Your daughter's home alone.'

Home alone. His daughter. Right. He'd forgotten.

From where they stood they'd hear her yell if she woke, he thought, but Gemma was right. His responsibility was to his daughter.

And Gemma's was to Milly.

The thought was so novel he was having trouble taking it in. But Gemma was calmly watching, waiting for him to go—so she could take over his responsibilities.

'I'll go, then.'

'You do that, Dr Ethan,' Gemma said calmly. 'I'll contact you if you're needed.'

It seemed that he'd been dismissed.

CHAPTER SIX

IT WAS two hours before Gemma felt confident enough of Milly to leave. Then Cady woke and she had to explain why there was a little girl in the next bed. There were introductions all round—Milly was so sedated that she wasn't aware of what was happening, but her parents were there and they'd lost enough of their terror to find some interest in another child.

Cady was bright-eyed and fascinated. He seemed to be improving by the minute and it took Gemma a while to get him back to sleep. Finally she was able to leave, with Milly's parents and the charge nurse maintaining watch.

She was *so* looking forward to bed, but as she walked through the connecting door into the darkened house beyond, she glanced into the sitting room. And there was Nate sitting in front of their Scrabble fire.

She hesitated. They'd had fun, she thought, and the lingering traces of their evening together still made her smile. So she stopped. There was one part of her that was screaming, Go right to bed. Do not pause. But the biggest part of her wanted to share the moment. Make him look at her rather than at the dying embers of the fire.

'Still pondering the rights and wrongs of ''flowery''?'

He looked up and he smiled and she thought, Yep, I know why I stopped. For that smile, well, any girl would pause.

'I know the wrongs of ''flowery'',' he told her darkly, and she chuckled.

'You're a sore loser.'

'Right.' He pushed himself to his feet and tilted the

Scrabble board so that the letters landed in a scrambled heap. 'OK. I concede that I've lost. Rematch tomorrow. Meanwhile how goes it?'

'She's good. As good as she can be for the attack she's had. She'll make it.'

'This time.'

'I'll teach her to swim. Starting as soon as she's over this scare. It's amazing how much difference it can make.'

It's amazing how much difference it can make. Nate thought that through. He knew what was making the difference. One slip of a girl. More and more the thought of her staying on seemed a really exciting prospect.

Medically exciting, he told himself. Hell, with her skills and expertise the possibilities were endless. She had to stay for more than two weeks. He had to persuade her.

But meanwhile she was watching him from the doorway, her head tilted slightly to one side in a look he was starting to know. And he knew suddenly that he wanted to detain her. Stretch out this moment—somehow. 'Can I make us some tea?'

'Nope. I need my bed.'

Nate was aware of a stab of disappointment. 'You don't want a rematch right now?'

'At one in the morning? No, thank you very much.'

But it wasn't just the time she was worried about, he thought. Her eyes were wary. She was holding herself apart.

'Hey, there's no need to look like that. I'm not going to jump you.'

'I never thought you would.'

But something was definitely bothering her. 'You know, I didn't jump your sister.'

Gemma sighed. 'I didn't think that either. I'm sure Fiona made the running. But...'

'But?'

'You did take her to bed. As I'm sure you've been taking Donna to bed—and I'm sure you've taken other women.'

He frowned. 'You think I should be saving myself?'

'No.' Her voice became suddenly clipped and hard. 'Of course I don't. I'm just saying that for you loving's easy.'

'And it's not for you?'

'No, Dr Ethan, it's not.' There was no mistaking her anger now and he felt a mounting anger in return. Who was she to judge him? What did she know of his love life?

And what did he know of hers? 'So Cady's all the family you ever intend to have?'

'That's right.'

'What's that got to do with me? Why does it make you angry?'

She stared at him and her eyes were suddenly baffled. What did it have to do with him? Nothing, she thought. Nothing at all. And why had she lashed out at him? And why was she even talking about where she wanted to go in life?

It was all too much. She was too tired to think this through. 'I'm going to bed.'

'Don't let me stop you.'

'Fine.' She glared but her glare didn't quite work.

'Gemma...' She'd walked part way into the room but was backing out now and she looked... For heaven's sake, she looked as if she was afraid of him. 'Don't...'

'Don't what?'

'Don't act as if I'm an ogre.'

'I'm not.'

'So if I walk towards you, you won't back away.'

'Of course not.' But as he stepped toward her it took a huge effort to keep her feet still. Her brain was screaming '*Run*'.

Her brain was stupid. Nate was no threat. Of course he was no threat.

He was close now—too close for comfort. So close that her heart was hammering in her chest like she'd just run a three-minute mile. Which was really, really stupid.

'Gemma...'

'What?' Why did she sound breathless?

'I told you. You don't have to be afraid of me.'

'I'm not.'

Nate lifted his hand and traced the fine line from the corner of her eye down to the side of her mouth. It was a feather touch. A touch of reassurance. Nothing more.

So why did it send a tremor right through her?

'Um... I need to go to bed.'

'Of course you do.' But he made no move to leave, and neither did she. He was right there. His chest was almost touching her breast. Behind them the last of the fire crackled and hissed, and it was crazily, wonderfully intimate. Crazy...

'Please...'

She wasn't sure what she was asking for. She was no longer sure she even knew what she was doing. All she knew was that he was right there by her, that he was big and warm and...and Nate.

Silence.

The silence went on and on, stretching into the night. Neither of them knew what it was that was being asked—or decided. All they knew was that there were currents running between them that were as old as time itself.

Time is. Time is yet to come.

Gemma knew what Nate was going to do before he did it. She guessed. Or rather she felt his intention in a part of her body that had nothing to do with consciousness. And everything to do with the need between a man and a woman.

He kissed her. How could he not? She was so...

He hardly knew what she was, but she was there, and her face was looking up at him, her eyes were wide with wonder and her expression was mutely waiting—wondering. And when he bent and kissed her it was like the coming together of two halves of a whole.

She was so sweet. She was so...right!

Gemma.

They knew each other not at all—yet so well. Each curve of their bodies fitted together with a sureness—a rightness that couldn't be argued with.

Nate felt his body stiffen in shocked recognition. He knew this woman. He knew her! His mind numbed as his mouth tasted the woman in his arms.

Because suddenly, shockingly, nothing had ever felt so right before.

And Gemma...

For a moment she didn't respond at all. She couldn't. And then, as though responding to a force beyond her understanding, she opened her mouth to him. But more than that.

She opened her heart...

Nate felt her lips move beneath his as her body melted into his. Chest against breast—man against woman—aching—wanting—welcoming, as a woman welcomed a man home after battle. Home to hearth and to heart.

There were forces at work here that neither could recognise—forces that were stronger than both of them.

Unconsciously Nate's hands fell to pull her body tighter against him—loving the way her breasts moulded themselves against his chest. His kiss deepened and so did the wonder. His mouth was tasting her—searching—wanting—seeking to know how this could be—that he'd found wonder in such a place. With such a woman.

The woman he was holding was like no woman he'd ever kissed. She felt…right.

Why? She was nothing like the other women he'd known! She wore no trace of make-up. Her clothes were stained and old, her hair twisted haphazardly into a hastily arranged braid, she was too thin, too tired, too weighed down by the encumbrances of her world.

How could she be filling this need—this need he'd never been aware he had?

In the end it was his shock that made him draw back— to pull away and hold her at arm's length to see what it was about her that was so amazing—to see who it was that he was holding. He hardly knew, and what he saw confused him still further.

She was such a slip of a thing—a waif. She held not a candle to the likes of Donna and Fiona.

What was he thinking of, kissing her? What had he done? She'd threatened to run because he'd tried to leave his baby with her. And now… Now he'd kissed her. Would she run now?

For a long, long moment they stared at each other, their confusion mirrored in each other's eyes.

'Gemma…' His voice was damnably unsteady. Hell, *he* was damnably unsteady.

'Don't…don't apologise,' she managed. Dear God, it needed only that. For him to kiss and apologise.

'I don't—'

'You don't understand. Good. That makes two of us.'

'I never meant…'

'And neither did I.'

'So…'

'So I'll go to bed.' Then, as he made to move toward her again—to gather her in his arms again because that was what they both wanted and he knew it—she held up her hands as if to fend him off. 'No.'

'But you want—'

'I don't know what I want,' she said in a jagged whisper. 'The only thing I do know is that I need to go to bed. Right now. You said you wouldn't jump me, Nate Ethan. You said Fiona did all the running. So why don't I believe a word you say?'

And that was it. She turned and ran down the corridor without a backward look.

Why did Gemma unsettle him so badly? What was it with the woman? And why the hell had he kissed her?

Nate lay awake almost until dawn. Hell, he usually slept like a log—but something about Gemma Campbell was getting under his skin.

Why?

She wasn't the sort of woman who usually interested him. He liked his women gorgeous and beautifully groomed and sort of cool…

Like Donna?

Yeah. Like Donna. He thought of her now, her svelte figure, her long manicured fingers, her oh, so carefully applied make-up.

Gemma didn't look as if she knew what make-up was. He'd seen her while she'd sat with Cady this evening, her face troubled and her blunted fingernails going to her mouth in a gesture of pure worry.

Why was she so worried? Cady would be fine—and he was only her nephew after all.

No. He was much more than that, Nate corrected himself. When Gemma gave her heart she gave it absolutely—and she'd given her heart to Cady. A mother couldn't have loved a child any more than Gemma loved her nephew.

Gemma…

He could still feel her in his hands. He could still taste her.

He still wanted her—damn, for some stupid reason he wanted her more than he'd wanted any woman in his life before.

Why?

There was a murmur in the crib beside him and he almost welcomed the interruption to his thoughts. Mia. He had worries of his own besides Gemma. Responsibilities.

He headed for the kitchen and made up a bottle, then returned to the bedroom to change and feed his baby. This was nappy number six and he was getting more proficient by the minute.

'We're doing OK,' he told his daughter, taking her back to the warmth of his bed for her feed.

But as he lay back in the darkened room with Mia in his arms he thought back to the expression he'd seen on Gemma's face when she'd cuddled Cady. She was a proper mother. She knew how to love her kid.

He'd love Mia, he thought.

But, damn, he wasn't as good at loving as Gemma was. What had she said?

For you loving's easy…

No, he decided. There lay the problem. It wasn't. Loving was hard. In fact, loving was something he didn't do. Sure, he'd had a multitude of girlfriends and a couple of them he'd come perilously close to marrying, but now…

Maybe he'd marry Donna.

Well, why not? This baby needed a mother.

But then he let himself think it through and it didn't seem such a good idea. In fact, it seemed like it would be a disaster. Marry Donna? He needed his head read. She'd run a mile rather than commit herself to a baby.

But if he promised marriage…

She just might do it, he thought. They'd been going out together for six months, she was in her early thirties and eager for the full bridal bit so maybe…

What was he thinking? Nate hauled himself back to reality with a jerk. Donna would make a perfectly appalling mother—and he didn't love her. And she'd be a wife for appearances. There was no depth...

He looked down at the baby in his arms and his own eyes stared reflectively back at him. He felt his stomach contract into a knot of something he hardly recognised.

Was he learning to love? Maybe he was. At the very least, he cared.

'You need a mother,' he told his little one, and let his thoughts drift back to Gemma. But he wasn't thinking of what he felt about her. He wasn't thinking of how she'd felt under his hands...under his mouth...

Somehow he blacked that out. Sort of. What she felt for Cady was what he wanted for his daughter, he decided. This wasn't about him. It was about Mia and he wanted that commitment.

'So maybe I'd better marry Gemma.'

Now, there was a thought. He grimaced—and then thought suddenly, Why not?

Because she'd laugh at the suggestion, he realised.

But if she didn't...

The taste of her lips came back to him—the sweetness of her. The moulding of her body.

'Cut it out. It's a practical idea only. It has nothing to do with my feelings.'

Marriage to Gemma...

'It's worth thinking about,' he told his daughter, and she smiled a windy half-smile—and burped her satisfaction with life in general.

And in the next room? Gemma lay awake staring at the ceiling and thought about what Nate had said. And thought about how Nate had felt.

Which was just plain wonderful.

'I know why you chose him as the father of your baby,' she said to the dark—to the shadows of her sister. 'If I was going down your road—suicide by childbirth—then maybe Nate would be the man I'd choose to be the father of my child.'

Which was crazy. The whole thing was crazy. Suicide by childbirth…

'If I'd had Nate then I'd· want to live.'

She didn't have Nate. She didn't have anyone. She hadn't been near a man since Alan, and what a disaster that had turned out to be. And now? One kiss did not a relationship make, and letting things go further than one stupid kiss wasn't an option.

I'd be a fool.

'So Cady's all the family you ever intend to have?' she asked herself, and the answer was right there, written in stone in the darkness above her head.

That's right. How can I do more?

But the thought was indescribably bleak. Indescribably lonely.

Why had she let herself be kissed? Why had she let herself fall—as Fiona had fallen?

Damn Fiona, she thought. Damn her, damn her, damn her. She'd done so much damage.

'She's dead now. She can't hurt you any more.'

Ha. Would she ever escape from the hurt Fiona had inflicted?

The thought of Nate's laughing eyes and his wonderful kiss came into her dreams and stayed there, infinitely sweet, infinitely tempting.

'Yeah. And dreams are all it is. There's no way someone like that would ever look at the likes of me. As for kissing…he'd kiss a broomstick if he thought it was female and wouldn't object.'

But in the next room, Nate was thinking of weddings.

'I think we might take Cady's drip out today.'

It was breakfast time. Gemma had hardly slept and there

were dark shadows under her eyes. Nate noticed but didn't comment. They were alone in the kitchen. Graham was relishing the fact that he wasn't needed medically so after an evening of playing the Major-General he'd decided to have a good sleep-in.

Which was what Gemma needed, Nate thought, wondering how he could bully her into it. He couldn't. He couldn't bully this woman into anything.

What lay between them—the memory of a kiss—was like a barrier, erected and in place until further notice.

'That's…that's great.'

What was great? He was distracted. What…?

Cady. Concentrate on Cady. Right.

'His sugars are down to eight this morning and still dropping. I think we can move to four insulin shots a day and start adjusting his dosage from there.'

'He'll hate the injections.'

'Kids adjust,' Nate said gently. 'The needles are tiny, and he's a smart enough kid to explain things to.'

'No four-year-old likes being hurt.'

'He's taken everything on the chin,' Nate told her. 'There hasn't been a tear, even when I've done the blood sugars. I think he's going to be fine.'

'Brave doesn't equate with fine.' She stared down at her toast and pushed it away. 'Brave just means we feel better—not Cady.'

'And not being brave means we don't eat our toast. Which is silly.' He pushed it gently under her nose again. 'Not brave means you don't measure up to Cady's standards. You look after yourself, Dr Campbell. It's the least you can do in the face of Cady's bravery.'

Gemma looked up at him and he smiled at her, and his smile was warm and caressing. And something more. Something she couldn't put her finger on.

Proprietorial?

Surely not. She was hallucinating here.

'I'm fine.' She chomped into her toast and promptly choked. Nate laughed and came around the table to thump her on the back.

'Not fine enough.'

'Thank you.' She spluttered on a mouthful of tea and turned a deep pink. What was it with this man? He had the power to make her act like a schoolgirl with a crush. Which she wasn't.

Was this a crush? No way.

'H-how's Milly?'

'Better. I think we might risk taking out the intubation tube this morning.' Taking out the tube was a delicate timing decision. If they took it out too early, they risked having to put it back in. But if they left it too long, it would further diminish the capacity of Milly's muscles to keep enough oxygen in her lungs.

'I was waiting to hear what you thought before I made a decision,' Nate told her, and she coloured again. He'd accepted her training with not a sign of reluctance. She'd worked alongside enough ego-driven young male doctors to know how rare his attitude was.

'I'll see her after breakfast.'

'How do you feel about running a surgery?'

Well, why not? She had to start some time. But there was a slight problem. 'As long as patients don't mind me as I am.' She motioned down to her distinctly grubby jeans and T-shirt. 'I'll admit this is hardly a confidence-inspiring uniform.'

'I think your problem might be solved. The station-master dropped a suitcase off this morning. It's in the hall.'

'My clothes!'

'That'd be it.'

'Great. Now I can feel normal.'

Only Gemma didn't. She changed into a sensible skirt and blouse with flat shoes, braided her hair into a sensible rope and headed for the surgery feeling stranger than she'd ever felt in her life. And when she met Nate the feeling intensified. He looked down at her clothes and his eyes creased in distaste.

'Is that the best you can do?'

'Is that the politest you can be?' she retorted.

'They're awful.'

'As opposed to, say, what Donna would wear?'

'As opposed to what anyone who's not on welfare would wear.'

'Yeah, well, that's nearly me.' She bit her lip. She knew these clothes were bad—her skirt was years old, her blouse was torn across the shoulder and she'd stitched it up, and her shoes—well, in fact, they had come from a welfare shop.

'You've been working as an anaesthetist for how long?'

'I've been fully qualified for three years.'

'Registrars are well paid even before they're qualified. That means you've been on a decent salary for well over five years. What gives?'

'It's none of your business.'

Wasn't it? Maybe not. But he really wanted to know.

'Gemma…'

'Look, my sister left debts,' she flung at him. 'My mother spent every penny she had on Fiona—there was nothing left when she died—and I married an absolute skunk who's cleaned me out for everything I owned and then some. If I work solidly for the next thirty years I may just clear my debts. Maybe.'

That stunned him. She was *married*?

'I didn't know…'

But it was a road she didn't want to travel with him. 'No,' she said in a voice that said any more enquiries were a waste of time. 'But a white coat hides a multitude of sins. So can we get on with it, please?'

'I guess…'

How come she'd been married?

Nate wanted to know. Desperately he wanted to know, but the more he saw of her the more she held herself aloof.

Was Gemma divorced?

It didn't matter. Or it shouldn't matter. As long as her previous marriage was over, she was available. And this *was* a good plan. Once he'd thought of marriage the idea wouldn't go away.

But…was she free? Or was she still married?

Damn, he had to find out. She had him intrigued.

Intrigued as opposed to interested, he told himself hastily. Since when had he ever been interested in drab little females with children in tow? No. He definitely wasn't interested.

But he was definitely intrigued.

And shabby or not, married or not, the patients loved Gemma. By the end of her first day in clinic Nate was hearing nothing but praise for his new partner. By the end of the week it was a ground swell.

'They want you to stay,' he told her as they sat down to dinner on Friday night. Graham was off being the Major-General, Nate had refused an invitation to go out to dinner with friends—Donna would be there and his current plans definitely didn't include Donna—and they were eating at home. With Cady and Mia asleep, it felt so domestic he could practically hear the theme from *The Brady Bunch* playing in the background.

'Who wants me to stay?'

'Everyone.' He looked across the table at his intended wife. She was a peaceful woman, he thought. She'd moved into their house and she may as well not have been there for all the trouble she caused. Cady was a quiet kid and she was quieter. She spoke when spoken to, kept herself to herself and at the end of the week he knew little more about her than he had at the start.

But there were things he wanted to know. Like—who was her husband?

But while his mind was flying off on tangents she was still back at thinking of the people who wanted her to stay. 'Including you?'

'Including me.' He smiled at her and wished that she'd smile back. She was too darned serious for his liking. 'Gemma, this week has been fantastic. We've done a full surgical list. We've been able to put two more nurses on and that's two more families with a second income—in this farming community that's wonderful. The hospital will go from strength to strength if you stay.'

'Mmm.' She still sounded noncommittal.

Damn, she had to stay. She must.

'And Graham's having the time of his life.' He pressed on, regardless of her lack of enthusiasm. 'He's seeing a few old patients every morning and the rest of the time he's free. Which is just the way he wants it. You must be able to see that he's feeling like the weight of the world's been lifted from his shoulders?'

She did see that. In the week since she'd been here she'd grown to like the old man very much. He was always around, his quiet good humour making the house a home as nothing else could. He and Cady had become fast friends and she'd often found them fishing in the river beyond the house, or sitting on the big old settee on the front veranda discussing the ills of the world—or just strolling around the little town hand in hand, taking in the gorgeous autumn weather. Kicking up autumn leaves together. Graham was the grandpa Cady had never had—could never have—and it warmed Gemma's heart to see them.

'He and Cady have become such good friends—and it's made a huge difference that Graham's diabetic,' she said softly, and Nate nodded.

'It has. Cady's already thinking that diabetes is normal.' The child and the old man solemnly tested their blood sugars together before each meal and then discussed how much insulin they should use with the gravity of village elders deliberating over events of state.

'It's been great.'

'So will you stay?'

Gemma looked doubtfully across the table and Nate thought, What? What?

'I don't know. I still have another week to make up my mind.'

'So what's stopping you making your mind up right now?'

'I don't know.'

'Is it the anaesthetics? Are you missing it?'

'No,' she said truthfully. 'There's enough call for my skills here to keep my hand in.' That much had already been proved. The local palliative care team were using her already and Nate knew that her skills at pain relief were far greater than his.

'So what, then?' He was watching her face, trying to read it. 'Is it me?'

'No. You're a good surgeon. A fine country doctor. It's been a pleasure to work with you.'

He nodded, trying to hide the surge of pleasure her

words gave him. 'Thanks. But I don't think it's my surgery we're talking about—is it?'

'No.'

'Then what?'

'You're Mia's father,' she said flatly, and he grimaced.

'You're still holding it against me—that your sister used me?'

'It's more than that,' she confessed, staring into the dregs of her teacup instead of at him. 'It's being around Mia. She looks like you but there's so much of Fiona in her.'

'You're afraid of loving her?'

'Yes.'

'Why?'

'Because how can I stay here for a year or two and then calmly walk away? Cady's already fond of her now. To pull them apart after a couple of years would be cruel. And...I'm not sure I could walk away either.'

'Then don't.'

'This isn't a lifetime offer,' she said flatly. 'Anything could happen in a couple of years. Graham could die. Without your uncle tying you to the place you may well decide to return to the city.'

'I won't.'

'There's more women...of your type...back in the city.'

His face darkened with anger. 'Hell, Gemma...'

She bit her lip. 'I'm sorry. That was uncalled for. But you know what I mean. You're a fish out of water here.'

'Meaning...'

'Meaning you love your social life. You love beautiful women. You're not a true country doctor.'

'How the hell would you know what a country doctor is? Who are you to judge me?'

'I'm not...I can't...' She sighed and rose to clear the table. 'I guess I don't know you at all. But that's just it. I don't know you, and if I agree to stay I'm putting my trust in you for the long term.'

'And you don't trust me?'

'No. I don't. You kissed me and I don't know why. I don't think you know why either. And what I don't understand I don't trust. I don't trust…people.'

He hesitated but then probed on. 'Life's been a disaster?'

'Apart from Cady. He's my one good thing.'

He sat and watched while she cleared away. He knew he should get up and help but he was watching her as she moved silently around the table. She looked like she'd been slapped, he thought. Over and over again. She looked like she was expecting it to continue into the future.

And his half-formed idea suddenly started to crystallise.

He thought about it as she stacked the plates. He thought about it as she started washing dishes—one plate, two, three, then the mugs…

And halfway through the crockery he could stand it no longer. She picked up the dishcloth, lifted a plate—and out it came.

'Gemma, what about if you married me?'

CHAPTER SEVEN

*W*HAT about if you married me…?

Gemma stood stock still—and then she dropped the plate.

'Excuse me?' It was hardly a whisper. Her face had gone chalk white.

'You heard.'

'No.'

Nate rose then and picked up the plate she'd dropped. It had split into two perfect halves. He put them in the trash and then turned to face her. Damn, she still had that expression on her face. Like she was expecting pain.

'I mean it.' His hands caught her shoulders and held. 'I've thought about this—'

'You don't know what you're saying.'

'I do. I'm asking you to marry me.'

'You don't even know me.'

'I do.' His eyes studied hers and what he saw there only served to confirm his views. 'I know you're loyal and true and caring. I know you love Cady to bits—and, despite everything she did to you, you loved your sister. I know you're hurt and you're tired and you've run out of places to run. So don't run any more. Stay here with us. For ever.'

She let herself look at him—really see him—and what she saw in his eyes astounded her. His hands were holding her but she was scarcely aware of the touch. She was only aware of his words. 'You're serious!'

'Never more so.'

'But… What about Donna?'

'Donna is…Donna was my girlfriend.'

'But it's normal…' Her voice faltered and died. She swallowed and tried again. 'It's normal to ask your girlfriend to marry you. Not a total stranger.'

'I thought about that. Donna won't do.'

'Won't do?'

'As a mother to my daughter.' There. The thing was out. This aching need.

'Is that what you want?' she whispered. 'A mother for Mia?'

'I want what Cady has,' he told her truthfully, knowing that nothing else but truth would do. 'I want that for Mia. I've watched you with Cady. You love him so much… OK, Mia is my daughter and I intend to give this love caper the best shot I can. Whether I succeed is a different matter. But, succeed or not, Mia needs a mother—and I'd like that mother to be you.'

Anger flared at that. 'You can't persuade me to take her any other way—so you offer marriage?'

But the grip on her shoulders tightened. 'No. Not just that. We can give each other so much.'

'Like…what?'

'Like a home.' His grip was becoming more urgent. Trying to make her see. 'What we have here is fantastic, but it's like you said. I could decide to leave. So could you, and we'd be tearing the kids apart. What they need is permanence, and a marriage would give them that.'

'You're out of your mind.'

'I'm not. I've been thinking about this for a week now.'

'Then you've been out of your mind for a week.'

'No. Look, Gemma, I don't know what sort of disaster your first marriage was…'

'It was some disaster.'

'There you go, then. You don't want to repeat the same mistake twice.'

'So why should I marry?'

'Because this time you'd be marrying with your head and not your heart.'

'Right. I see.' But she was still looking at him as if he was crazy and her voice said she was humouring a lunatic.

But he wasn't intending to stop now. 'It'd be good for all of us.'

'Tell me why.'

'Right.' Reluctantly he let her go—as if he feared she might take the opportunity and make a bolt for it. The expression in her eyes said that she was thinking about just that. 'First there's Graham.'

'OK, What about Graham?'

'He needs to continue what he's doing—winding down his practice until he's just seeing his favourite patients. You can see how much he needs it. These few days have been magnificent but he's already worrying about keeping up his skills. While there's the slightest risk that you'll leave, he won't let go. But if we were permanent he could work as little as he wants to, and spend some time with his...well, they'd be his pseudo-grandkids. You must see how much he'd enjoy that.'

Gemma could. She did.

'Then there's the kids. They'd be raised as brother and sister. How good would that be?'

It'd be fantastic. She could see that, too. 'But—'

'Then there's you.' Nate's tone gentled. 'Gemma, I don't know what sort of private hell you've lived in for the last few years, but by your face I can begin to guess. It wasn't just Fiona who treated you badly. Was it?'

She thought of her mother. And Alan. 'No, but—'

'But I'd never treat you badly,' he told her, and his tone was still so gentle she had to blink back disbelief and swallow threatening tears.

She believed him. She believed him!

'And then there's me.'

'Now, that's the part I don't understand,' she told him, trying frantically to get a grip on things. 'You could marry anyone you want.'

'I don't want.'

'But you will. You'll fall in love.'

'I won't.'

'Why?' She was close to hysteria here. 'Oh, for heaven's sake, why? You're not gay, are you?'

He grinned at that, his lovely deep chuckle rolling over her confusion. 'No, Gemma, I'm not gay.'

'Then what—'

'I nearly did marry once,' he told her. 'Marianne was another medical student and you should have seen her. She was the most gorgeous thing. I fell head over heels—at the ripe old age of nineteen. And I would have married her in all honour but she took off with my best man two days before the wedding. Can you believe that?'

Nate was smiling, but Gemma looking up at him saw the hurt beneath the laughter. It was a joke now—but it hadn't been a joke then and it had left a scar so deep that it was with him still.

'Oh, Nate, I'm sorry.'

'You needn't be. I had one more foray into a serious relationship and that, too, was a disaster. So I made a vow. No marriage. No commitment.'

'So what's changed?'

'I wouldn't be marrying for me. I'd be marrying for all of us. It makes a difference.'

'And if the likes of Donna comes along…'

'I've sown my wild oats,' he said, and the tone of virtue in his voice made her want to smile. Sort of. 'But it won't hurt me to become a family man and this house is big enough for us to lead separate lives.'

Oh, great. What sort of marriage was that?

'Nate, that's not—'

'I haven't finished yet,' he told her, his voice growing more certain. 'I know you need marriage. I know I can help.'

'You don't know anything about me.'

'You're in trouble financially.'

'I'm not.'

'Pull the other leg. It plays "Jingle Bells". Gemma, I want to talk to my accountant—and my lawyer—about your affairs. I'm sure you shouldn't be carrying your sister's debts into eternity. I can fix things.'

'You can't—'

'As your husband I damn well can.'

She blinked. He sounded bossy. Bossy but...nice.

And suddenly it was really, really tempting. To lay her troubles on this man's broad shoulders.

But he didn't know what he was taking on. And she... She at least knew what marriage could be. For a while there—for a minuscule window of time—she'd thought she'd had it. With Alan...

Only she'd woken up to the brutal truth too soon. And then Fiona had done what Fiona had always done.

Fiona. It was always Fiona.

And Alan was still with her, a nightmare waiting in the wings.

'I don't think you know what you'd be letting yourself in for,' she said gently, but he shook his head.

'I know. Permanence. Couldn't we all do with some of that?'

Permanence. She didn't know the meaning of the word.

'No.'

'At least think about it.'

'I've thought about it, and if you push it I'll have to leave. Because the whole idea's crazy.'

'It's not.'

'Ha!'

'Are you reluctant because I kissed you?'

'Why on earth…?'

'There wouldn't need to be that in our marriage—unless you want another baby.'

He actually sounded hopeful! The whole thing was so crazy she almost laughed. But not quite.

'There's easier ways to get yourself a locum than by marrying,' she told him bluntly. 'Advertise in the *Gazette*.'

'And get the likes of Fiona again? No, thank you very much.'

'Because you might end up with another baby.' She gazed at him for a long moment and then sighed. Really gut-wrenchingly sighed. As if she was almost tempted—but there was no way on earth she could take this gigantic leap of faith. 'Nate, I'm sorry.'

'You won't consider it?'

'No.'

'I'll change your mind. If you stay on. You'll see what sort of exemplary husband and father I can be.'

'Well, start now, then. There's no time like the present.' Gemma was suddenly angry. She tossed the dishcloth at him, hard enough to catch him across the face, and he was so surprised it slipped to the floor before he could catch it. 'Dry the dishes and put them away. And then play with your daughter. Or do the laundry. Do anything you like—unless it has to do with blackmailing me into taking on your domestic duties. Because I'm not doing it, Nate. I'm not that stupid.'

He'd messed it up. Gemma thought he wanted a domestic servant, he decided ruefully as he brooded over her refusal. He didn't. He wanted an equal.

But…it would be nice if she took over the things he didn't want to do. His fantasy was of a wife like his mother had been—Gemma walking the kids to school, Gemma reading to the kids before tucking them in at night. Gemma being there for them as he couldn't be.

Why couldn't he be?

Because he was the doctor, he thought. The bread-winner.

Damn, Gemma was a doctor, too. Her qualifications were every bit as good as his.

His fantasy was of her helping him—taking the load off his shoulders—making practice in this tiny town a pleasure instead of the burden it had become.

And in return he could help her out of her financial difficulties. He could...

His thought hit an obstacle there. What else could he do?

Hmm.

It was a bit of a one-sided coin, Nate conceded. But... she was so weary. She was so darned stressed. You'd think she'd fall on his offer just to share her load.

Was he offering to share her load? Or extend it?

He needed to find out what was going on in her back-ground, he decided. If there was still a husband then who was he and why had he left Gemma so burdened? What were her debts?

He needed to know more—and to keep her here until he knew.

'So no more proposing,' he told himself firmly. 'And no more kissing. Because she'll run a mile and this may well be the best chance you've got of getting yourself a sensible wife and mother for Mia.'

A sensible wife and mother...

Gemma knew exactly what Nate was asking—and why. Sensible Gemma. Hadn't she always been that?

Her earliest memories had been of being the sensible one. Gemma, who'd always taken second place to Fiona.

Gemma, who'd stayed home and done the housework while her mother had taken Fiona to one beauty pageant after another. Gemma, who had never been able to go on school trips because all the money had had to be used for Fiona—for Fiona's ballet lessons and deportment lessons and make-up and clothing... Gemma, who had worn Fiona's cast-offs right up until the moment Fiona had died.

Gemma, putting everything aside—interrupting her medical studies for a year to nurse her grandfather because her mother had refused to do it. That had been the year Fiona had almost become Miss Australia, and who could have stayed home and nursed an old man when that had been happening?

Then her mother had become ill herself. Fiona hadn't helped. Of course she hadn't.

Then taking on Cady... And trying to back away from Alan.

And finally the awful time spent nursing Fiona as she'd neared death.

Yep, that was Gemma all right. The sensible one. And here was Nate asking her to be that all over again.

Well, he could take a hike. She should leave right now.

But... Cady was so happy. Every day he was regaining his health. Mrs McCurdle and Graham thought he was the best thing since sliced bread—they were spoiling him rotten and they were just what he needed. Every time she decided to pack her bags and leave she'd hear Cady's delicious chuckle and she'd pause.

It was so unfair.

There was a part of her that whispered that Nate's offer would be so easy to accept. So...sensible. Make this arrangement permanent by marriage, and cope with the consequences later.

But she couldn't marry—even if she wanted to. How on

earth would Alan react? She daren't let herself think about it.

But the consequences were already with her.

'I've fallen in love with the man,' she whispered into her pillow, and the knowledge was as bitter as gall. Damn. Damn, damn and damn.

And a few more words besides.

'I don't swear. I never swear so why am I lying here making my pillow blush?

'It's Nate. He's got me so confused I don't know who I am any more.

'So marry him.

'As if that'd solve anything. As if you could, even if you wanted to. You've got rocks in your head, Gemma Campbell. The likes of Nate Ethan aren't for the likes of you. You'd give him your heart on a plate and he's already made it perfectly clear that he doesn't want it. He only wants Gemma the workhorse.'

Gemma the workhorse turned over and punched her pillow so hard a clump of feathers came sailing out of the lining and landed on her nose. She sneezed, and even smiled.

But she wasn't smiling when she finally fell asleep.

Nate found Gemma in the pool.

Every morning since Milly had been released from hospital Gemma had taken her into the pool and was patiently teaching her to swim. She'd had five lessons now and it was hard to say who was most pleased—Milly or her proud mother, who was beaming and beaming as she watched the lesson from the poolside.

As Nate walked into the poolroom Mrs Jefferson bounced up from the bench where she'd been watching. Milly's mother was practically bursting with excitement.

'She did five strokes on her own. Five strokes! Can you

believe that? And two weeks ago we thought we'd lost her.'

Nate looked in the water and Gemma and Milly were as flushed with triumph as Sandra Jefferson.

'That's great.'

'Do you want to see, Dr Ethan?' Milly called, and without waiting for a response she dived underwater. Her tiny arms splashed the water—*six* times—and when she surfaced she was beaming with triumph.

'That's six. That's six!'

If I'd told her to try and hold her breath that long to build her lung capacity, she would've stared at me blankly, Nate thought. There were miracles happening here.

'Now my lesson's finished, Cady's coming in with me,' Milly told him.

He knew that. That was why he was here. Mrs McCurdle had been dressing Cady in his swimming trunks when Nate had stopped for an early lunch, and he'd been unable to resist.

'You've got your bathers on, too,' Milly shrieked, pointing at Nate. He was wearing his trunks. 'Look! Look, Dr Campbell. Dr Ethan's coming in, too.'

Gemma looked—and saw.

She didn't look exactly delighted, Nate thought. She didn't look exactly anything.

Or maybe that wasn't the truth. Sure, she was wearing an ancient costume which looked like it'd fit a woman twice her size. It was stretched out of shape with age and the colour was indeterminate. But she was flushed with pride and she was smiling at the little girl in the water beside her. And, Nate thought suddenly, she has…something. An indescribable something. Not the stunning good looks of Fiona or Donna but a sort of magnetism…

He was dreaming.

Then Cady came bursting through the door, towing Mrs McCurdle behind him. When he saw Milly and Gemma in the water he yipped in excitement.

'Can you cope on your own?' Nate quizzed Gemma, and she smiled and flushed.

'I... Yes.'

'You wouldn't like some help?'

There was only one answer to that. 'I'd love some help.'

'Right.' And he dived in feeling suddenly, crazily joyful. Like the sun had just come out.

Because of Milly, he told himself.

Yeah, right.

What followed was one very silly, very happy half-hour. Two kids and two adults in the pool, with Mrs McCurdle and Sandra Jefferson watching indulgently from the side.

'You'd think they were children themselves,' Mrs McCurdle said placidly. 'Look at the pair of them. There'll be wedding bells in town soon—you mark my words.'

'I'm not disagreeing,' Sandra told her. 'It's obvious they're in love. It's just... I wonder if they've realised it yet.'

They hadn't realised anything of the kind. When the two women disappeared, bearing reluctant children with them, Nate and Gemma were left in the pool together. It was like being in the bath together, Gemma thought. It was too darned intimate for words.

'I should get out. I'm turning into a prune.'

'I'll bet you're not.' He was floating two feet from her nose. 'You look pretty good from where I'm floating.'

'My nose isn't wrinkled. But you should see my toes.'

For answer he duck-dived—straight underneath her. She felt his hand on her toe and yelped and splashed for the poolside.

'What do you think you're doing?'

'Nope,' he said, surfacing with laughter. 'You're not wrinkled. Ticklish, though—definitely ticklish.'

'Go away.'

'I'm away.' He was, too. A whole six feet. 'Seriously, Gemma—'

'You're not serious. You're never serious.'

'I am now. And what you're doing for Milly...it's a minor miracle.'

'She's responding better than I'd hoped.'

'You're building her lung capacity almost while we watch.'

'I hope it helps.'

'I'm sure it will.'

There was silence then. There seemed nothing left to say. He should get out, Nate thought. This had been a spur-of-the-moment decision—to take a swim—and he had patients waiting. So did Gemma.

But neither of them moved—yet.

'You haven't reconsidered...?'

And that broke the silence in no uncertain terms.

'No, I have not!' It was a snap and Nate grimaced. He should learn when to shut up.

'It's just...it's going so well.'

'Yes, it is. So why mess it up with talk of marriage?'

Why indeed? Nate hardly knew.

'I only thought—'

'Well, don't think. Thinking's dangerous. I never do it unless it's absolutely necessary.'

'So how do you operate?' he asked, fascinated. 'Without thinking?'

'I operate on gut instinct. Take Milly. It was a gut feeling that swimming would be good.'

'Gut feeling backed up with ten years of solid medical training.'

'There is that.'

'And what does your gut say about us?'

'My gut says your idea is crazy.'

'My gut says it'd work.'

'Well, there you go, then,' she said equitably. 'We have incompatible guts. What better reason for refusing a marriage proposal?'

'Gemma...'

'Knock it off, Nate,' she said. 'We have work to do. Stop wasting time.' And she put her head down and stroked out for the steps, strong and sure, leaving him to watch her with ever-increasing confusion.

They had more work to do than they bargained for. At five that afternoon, just as the lines in the surgery were starting to thin, there was a call from the local police.

'There's been a plane crash,' Nate told Gemma, putting his head around her consulting-room door as she wrote a script for Ruby Sawyer, an old lady with Parkinson's disease and an avid interest in the new doctor. 'It's just been rung in. The local police sergeant is on his way there now. All he knows is that it came down in a paddock near Millhouse's dairy. It might be a false alarm—nothing but a forced landing—but there might be work for both of us. If Graham takes over here, can you come?'

Could she come? A plane crash... 'Of course.' She grimaced apologetically at Ruby—whose expression said she'd love to come, too—and was out of her chair before Nate could close the door. She caught him as he was climbing into his car.

'What sort of plane?

He cast her a look that said he'd expected her to follow in her own car—not be ready in time to come with him. But he was glad that she had. This sounded as if it could be a nightmare. 'It's a light plane. Bob, our local police sergeant reckons it might be a Cessna. He got a call from a farmer's wife a mile away saying she saw it come in low and then heard a crash.'

'If she heard a crash from a mile away… Dear God…'

'I don't think it'll be pretty.'

It wasn't.

During the last two weeks Gemma hadn't once regretted leaving her life in the big city. She regretted it now. Nate pulled up at the gate leading to the dairy. Gemma gazed in horror at the wreck of the plane and thought longingly of all the medical services she'd left behind at Sydney Central.

Where were the fire engines? The ambulances? The paramedics? Where were the cranes and the specialist tow trucks? Where was…everybody?

There was one lone man—the local police sergeant, by the look of his uniform—spraying the smouldering ruin with a fire extinguisher far too small for the job.

Where was the cavalry?

'Hell, if it goes up in smoke…' Nate said grimly, and hauled an extinguisher from the back seat. 'Bring my bag, Gemma.' And he was off at a run, leaving Gemma to follow.

She brought up the rear but not at a run. She didn't hurry. She'd learned in her time as an emergency intern that if things weren't staring her in the face as immediately life-threatening then it was worth taking the time to do an overall assessment. Triage had been drilled into her as a medical student—the sorting of priorities.

Preventing a fire must be the first priority but there wasn't another fire extinguisher. Which left her free to take stock.

The plane looked as if it had been crop-dusting. A bright sign was still decipherable on its crumpled side. BUZZEM

WEEDS. The sign looked absurdly incongruous where it was.

It had crashed right into the dairy, smashing the whole structure. The plane itself was lying upside down on the sheets of galvanised iron that had once been the dairy roof.

Why had it crashed? Surely it hadn't been heading straight for the dairy. She looked further back from where it must have approached.

And there it was. The reason the plane had crashed. Three hundred yards from the dairy was a row of power lines. Or what had been a row of power lines. The plane had dropped too close to the wires, a pole had been hauled down and the cables were now trailing uselessly on the ground between pole and dairy.

Power lines...

She shouted to Nate, putting all the force she had into her yell. He turned and she pointed to the cables. She didn't know where they ended or whether they were still live.

Nate recognised her fear at a glance. He grabbed the policeman, signalling to the wires, and they moved away. There was one thing she could do. She lifted her cellphone and dialed the emergency number.

'There's a plane crash two miles north of Terama on the Black Hill road. I need the power cut. Now.'

They could do it, she thought. One central switch could well stop a further disaster.

But...

The operator was inept. 'I'm not sure...' She sounded flustered. 'It's after five... I'll have to try and find their emergency number.'

'Do it.'

But the need was now, not after the operator had located some vaguely contactable repairman. The cables were strewn right into the crash site.

She couldn't trust them. One step wrong and they'd be fried. So…

'Turn the damned power off,' she told herself as she slammed shut her phone.

'How?

'Learn by experience,' she told herself grimly. 'The hard way.' She looked around and found a tree branch—a piece of cypress about eight feet long—and walked toward the power lines like someone would have walked toward a cobra.

At least the wood was dry. If it had been raining the thing would have been impossible, but her branch seemed shrivelled and well dead. She knew enough to figure there shouldn't be any moisture to conduct electricity.

'Gemma…' Nate yelled across at her and she waved as she heard the alarm in his voice. He'd seen what she was doing.

'I'm just checking the lines.'

'Don't—'

But he didn't have a choice. He couldn't leave what he was doing. There were flames flickering at the edges of the crashed aircraft and if the fire hit fuel…

Would two extinguishers be enough?

The responsibility for the power lines was all Gemma's.

And somehow she did it. Walking carefully, approaching from behind and pushing the tangle of cables out of the way with her branch, she finally reached the pole. There were switches. About ten of the things…

She didn't trust that the pole itself wasn't live. Thinking fast, she tugged off her shoe. It had a rubber sole—surely she should be safe if she kept that between herself and any electricity source. Slipping her hand into its depths she leaned forward and flicked switches. One after another she switched, until all were in the 'up' position.

Gloriously, they had notations emblazoned on the plastic surface.

ON. And OFF. And now every single one of them was pointing to OFF.

She'd done it.

They'd still be unwise to trust them if they didn't have to—to stand on the cables—but she could hope now that they could approach the wreckage with safety. It was a calculated risk but worth it if there were lives to save.

Were there?

Gemma turned back to assess the damage.

The plane had smashed squarely into the dairy. There were forty or so cows lined up ready to be let in the gate. Milking hadn't started yet so there were no cows in the bales—or what had been cow-bales. The bales were crushed under the collapsed roof and the cows were huddled by the gates to the yard, an uneasy, restless herd.

So what was there?

She couldn't see. There were smouldering ruins—the dairy had collapsed in on itself and, apart from that one garish painted panel, the plane was just about unrecognisable.

No one could have survived that crash.

Or could they? Was anyone underneath?

She grabbed Nate's bag and took it over to where the two men were still spraying foam.

'Don't we have a fire service?'

'The brigade should be here any minute,' the policeman told her. 'Damned fire brigade... They have their practice every Friday night and I always say if you have to have a fire then don't have it on a Friday night.'

He glanced at the smouldering ruin and swore. 'Hell.'

'Who's in there?' Nate asked, his face as grim as the policeman's.

'It'll be Hector Blainey,' the policeman said, his face as grim as death. 'It's his plane. He's not walking out of this.'

'No.' Nate edged nearer, keeping an eye on the cable.

'I think the electricity's off,' Gemma said. 'I switched off everything I could see.'

If it wasn't dead the whole site would be live. They had to take the chance. 'I'll go in,' Nate said, edging over the mound of rubble toward the plane.

'Damn it, Doc… Wait for the brigade.'

'What will they do that I can't? It seems solid enough.'

It seemed no such thing. The pile of rubble looked as if it could come down any minute.

But Nate didn't stop. Carefully he picked his way across the mass of shattered bricks and mortar to the edge of the plane. He hauled away a section of what had once been the dairy roof and then ripped off the garish panel. What he saw there made him recoil.

'Hell.'

There was no need to ask what had caused his revulsion. For the pilot death must have been instantaneous.

'One?' Gemma asked, feeling as sick as Nate looked, and he nodded.

'I can only see the one—and it's Hec. He wouldn't have had any passengers if he was crop-dusting.'

'He shouldn't have been crop-dusting so low,' the policeman muttered, staring around him. 'What the hell was he doing, coming in so low over a dairy? He must have known the yard would be full. He'll have known he stood every chance of spooking the cows.'

'Which is probably just why he'll have done it,' Nate said, still staring around at the mess of what had once been the dairy. 'Hector and Ian Millhouse—the farmer who owns this dairy,' he explained for Gemma's benefit, 'have a long-standing feud. A boundary dispute.'

'Seems a damned high price to pay for a fight over a

bit of fence,' the policeman muttered, and Gemma could only agree.

'So where's Ian?' Nate's voice was still grim. He stood looking around him. 'If the cows are lined up for milking, he'll be here. Where…?'

And then he heard it. A faint moan coming from beneath the rubble where he was standing. Nate shifted sideways and stared down.

'Damn. He's beneath the plane. Give us a hand.'

The fire brigade arrived then—finally—with five volunteers on board. After confirming that Gemma had indeed turned the electricity off, one man took over playing water over the site—cooling everything down. Then they started hauling away bricks, the timber that had been the walls, sheets of galvanised iron still hot to touch…

Until the path to the iron under the plane was clear.

One of the men had a flashlight. He directed the beam underneath the iron in the direction the sound had come from, shining it in under the mess of roofing iron.

And then he whistled. 'Got him.'

They could see him. But they couldn't reach him.

The roofing iron formed a plate over the rubble that had been the dairy, and almost the full weight of the plane was holding it down.

They could see Ian's arm and part of his head—one side of his face. He was eight or ten feet under the iron, the iron seemed to be almost resting on top of him and he looked firmly trapped.

Hell!

It was hell. He was so far in—and he was almost directly underneath the plane. It was a wonder he was alive at all.

'Ian, can you hear me?' Nate called, and there was another groan in response. And then…

'Doc…'

'Yeah, it's me.' Nate's voice was grim. 'What's going on, Ian? Are you stuck?'

'Yeah. There's a ruddy big sheet of iron holding me. And I can't...I can't feel my legs. Can't move them.'

'You wouldn't want to. With this mess around the wisest course is to keep still.'

But Nate was looking at Gemma and their eyes reflected their fear. Why couldn't he feel his legs?

'There's blood...damn it, Doc, I'm bleeding like a stuck pig. My head...'

'Ian, listen to me. This is important. Can you put a hand on the source of the bleeding?'

'I... Yeah...' But his voice was fading.

'Put as much pressure on the source of the bleeding as you can,' Nate told him. 'We'll be with you just as soon as possible.' Then he turned to the people around him. 'We have to get that plane off.'

'And how the hell are we going to do that?' The fire chief wasn't very bright at the best of times and he was looking at Nate for guidance.

'We need a crane. A big one.'

'It'll have to come from Blairglen.'

'Then get on the radio and get it here,' Nate snapped. 'Fast.'

'It'll be at least an hour.'

'An hour's better than nothing. Move!'

But...an hour was impossible. Numb legs and a bleeding head wound... An hour would be far too long.

'We can't leave him under there for that long,' Gemma said, and Nate shook his head.

'We don't have a choice. If we try to move things while the plane's still there, we risk the whole thing coming down on top of him. As it is...let's work with shoring timbers and see how far in we can get.'

'But you won't be able to get under the plane. If you

try and raise the iron, the whole thing might tip—or just crumple.'

'Well, what else do you suggest?'

'That I go in.' She tilted her chin and met his look of startled surprise. 'Nate, there's twelve inches' or more space between the iron and the rest of the rubble. If we can see him then I can reach him.'

'You're kidding.' Nate looked blank.

'I know the gap's too narrow for you or any of the guys, but I'm the thinnest of the lot of you. I think I'll fit.'

'Gemma...'

But she was thinking it through out loud. 'The brigade will have ropes. They can attach a couple round me, then when I'm in there I can haul in stuff that I need—and you can pull me out if you have to.'

'And if the lot settles...'

'It won't. It looks solid enough.'

'It doesn't look anything of the kind. It could come down at any time' he said explosively. 'Gemma, I can't allow it.'

'And how are you going to stop me?' Already she was on her knees, peering under the iron—then moving to lie on her back so she was looking at Nate face up, half in and half out of the iron. 'Do you have any other ideas?'

'You can't—'

'Tell me—if the iron was three inches higher would you be going in?'

Nate didn't hesitate. A man was dying. 'Yes, but—'

'Well, there you go, then.'

'But you have Cady.'

'And you have Mia. And I'll bet Ian has kids—doesn't he?'

He stared at Gemma with desperation in his eyes, but she was demanding the truth. 'Three.'

'Well, there you are. Just…if anything goes wrong, look after Cady. Promise?'

There was nothing else to say. 'I promise.'

'Put on overalls and a hard hat,' the fire chief ordered, seeing the impossibility of further argument. He was handing over his own equipment and then stood back, baffled. Like the rest of the men. This was a chit of a girl. It seemed so wrong—that she put herself in danger while they stood back and did nothing.

'Hell, Gemma…' Nate looked ill.

'I'll be fine.'

But as she hauled on her overalls Nate stooped and touched her—a feather touch on the forehead. It was a tiny gesture and only Gemma knew what it truly meant.

It was a blessing. And a prayer.

Nate would be in my shoes if he could be, she thought. He was desperate to be doing what she was doing.

To be honest, she wasn't all that thrilled about doing it herself.

But needs must. Under the iron there was a man who could well be bleeding to death.

'They didn't warn us about this type of thing when we enrolled for medical school,' she said lightly as she stuck her hard hat on her head. 'Sometimes accountancy or kindergarten teaching or cleaning lady look like really attractive professions.'

It was time to go. Gemma looped her ropes around her waist and slid her body under the iron.

CHAPTER EIGHT

IT WAS hot and exceedingly wet. These were the first things Gemma noticed. The men had used extinguisher foam to prevent the place going up in smoke and then they'd played water over the iron to cool it. But the iron was buckled and twisted and torn, and the water had seeped through. It stank now of the aviation fuel it was mixed up with. The cavity was vilely uncomfortable and it was incredibly claustrophobic.

'If you were thinking of having a cigarette while you wait for me, maybe you should think again,' she gasped as she hauled herself ever so carefully towards the farmer.

'Holy heck.' Weak to the point of death or not, Ian sounded as if he couldn't believe what he was hearing. 'It's a woman!'

'Now, don't tell me a woman's place is in the kitchen,' she told him, wiggling under a jagged piece of iron that was almost as low as her nose. 'Otherwise I'll be forced to go make you a nice batch of scones instead of rescuing you.'

'You're...rescuing me?' His voice sounded a long way away. Like he was concentrating on pain rather than what was happening around him. Really bad pain.

'Someone has to do the rescuing.' Keep it light, Gemma told herself. She was trying desperately not to let fear pervade her voice but it was damnably hard. 'What do they say? Behind every successful man there's a woman? And in cases like this, the woman's right out in front. Because the woman's the only one who'll fit.' She tried to keep her voice light and confident—no easy task when there were bits of iron sticking into her legs, a splinter had just rasped her cheek and the smell of the spilled fuel was over-powering. 'How are you doing?' She'd worked her way six feet under the iron. Another eight or so to go...

'Not...not too good.'

'Do you know who I am? I'm the lady doctor.'

'I heard about you.' It was a huge effort for the farmer to talk, she thought. He was drifting toward unconscious-ness.

She had to stop talking. Shoving her way though the mass of crumpled iron and wood took all her concentra-tion.

'Are you OK, Gemma?' Nate was shining the fireman's flashlight past her, trying to light her way, but the gap was too narrow and the flashlight's battery was fading. His voice sounded sick with anxiety.

'I'm fine.'

She wasn't the least bit fine. The fumes were making her head dizzy and she felt sick.

But somehow she kept going. Somehow...

And finally she reached Ian—just. By stretching out, her fingers could fleetingly touch his face. It was contact as welcome for Gemma as it must have been for the farmer. 'Hey, Ian, don't you dare go to sleep on me. Not when I've crawled all the way in to say hello.'

'I don't...'

'You don't even know my name.' She pushed against a piece of timber blocking her path. It moved—just a bit—but the iron above it didn't seem to shift so she pushed it down toward her legs. She gained another couple of splin-ters in the process but it gave her a clear passage. 'I'm Gemma.'

'I'm Ian.'

'That's great.' She now had clear access. She let her hand drift over his face until she found what she was looking for. There was a steady pumping of blood from his forehead. 'Let's get this stopped.'

At least she'd known to expect this. She had a wad of dressing roped against her waist. Now she hauled it up and pushed it as hard as she could against his head. She could feel the blood pulsing under her hand. It was a filthy gash, she thought grimly. Deep and jagged and ripped into more blood vessels than she cared to imagine.

It was just as well she was here. He wouldn't last for an hour without her.

But would he last for an hour with her?

It was almost impossible to adjust a pressure bandage in these conditions. The flashlight was fading and she was working almost blind. She bound tape around the farmer's head and tightened it until she could tighten no further— and then she had to feel with her fingers whether the flow was easing.

And blessedly it was. 'Yes!'

It was a minor triumph. The big farmer was slipping toward unconsciousness. 'I feel so… Geez, Doc, I think I have to sleep…'

'Don't you dare sleep on me,' she ordered. 'There's forty cows out there depending on you. They're hanging their heads over the gate right now waiting for your ugly face to appear.'

'They'll want milking.'

'I reckon someone else might milk tonight.' Heck, she was losing him. The pulse under her hand was fast and weak. 'Nate…'

Nate was waiting, crouching back a little from the entrance to her cavern so as not to block the little light she had. 'Gemma.' There was no hiding the anxiety in his voice.

'Ian's legs are stuck fast. There seems to be some sort

of beam over them—I can't see to tell you more. I need
saline and plasma. And morphine.'

'You can administer them while he's in there?'

She didn't have a choice. There was a deep pool of
blood under her hand and the farmer's head was still ooz-
ing.

'Of course I can,' she managed, her tone far more confident than she felt. 'What's a little confinement and darkness to a beaut anaesthetist like me? Can you send in what
I need?'

'Can do.' They'd rigged the rope around her waist in a
loop, so that as she tugged her equipment along the cavity
toward her, the other side of the loop returned to the outside world. It was a makeshift supply line but it would
have to do.

Damn it, it must.

'And I need a decent flashlight.' This one was all but
dead and she had to be able to see what she was doing.
Surely firefighters carried torches.

These firefighters didn't. 'Ron...do we have a decent
torch?' she heard Nate ask the fire chief, and by the sound
of his expletive she knew the response had been a helpless
shake of the head.

'There's one up at the house,' the farmer muttered. 'In
the back porch.'

'Did you hear that?' Gemma asked, and heard Nate
swear again as he relayed the information to those behind
him.

'Yes, I want you to find it.'

He'd heard—but he was dealing with morons.

'They're going now,' he told her.

Gemma thought, Good—if two of them went then
maybe combined they might just have enough brain power
to find the torch.

Meanwhile...

'I need to rip your shirt,' she told the farmer. She was working one-handed—the other was still applying pressure to his head.

'Don't mind me—it's not my Sunday best.'

'Great.'

It was thick flannel—much worse than his Sunday best, Gemma thought, as it was much stronger—but somehow she did it. She released the pressure on his head for a fraction of a second, put her teeth into the cloth and ripped. It was a small triumph but it was enough to give her a boost. It was wonderful what you could do when you had to!

And then there was a call from the outside world and Nate was shining a new flashlight in to light the darkness.

'I'm sending this in, Gem.'

Gem... Her grandfather had called her Gem, she thought inconsequentially. Once upon a lifetime, he'd called her that and she'd loved it. It was a term of endearment that hadn't been used since he'd died.

And why it had the capacity to pull her off stride here...

Not for long. She had herself together soon enough, hauling the syringes and packs of saline and plasma toward herself. Nate had rigged up the flashlight so it bobbed along with the supplies, lighting their path. It meant that when they caught on an obstacle he and Gemma could see what was happening. Holding one end of the loop each, they could wiggle it past.

Finally she had what she needed. All she had to do was set it up. Easier said than done.

'What sort of feeling do you have in your legs?' she asked, and the farmer gave a weary grunt.

'Pins and needles.'

Well, that was something. Better by far than the nothing he'd reported earlier. If he'd received a blow to his spine he could have temporary nerve damage and the pins and needles might be a sign that they were recovering.

'I like pins and needles,' she told him warmly. 'It means you're getting your circulation back.'

'All the better to bleed with.'

He could joke. Great.

Now all she had to do was get fluids aboard—rebuild his blood supply—and hope like crazy they could get him out without any further damage.

It was a long, long wait.

Getting the plasma and saline running was a nightmare. She needed room, she needed drip stands, she needed nurses to hold equipment... In fact, what she needed was a hospital. But, somehow, working by the light of the torch and manoeuvring through dust and wreckage and the stench of spilled fuel—somehow she managed it. It had been the most non-sterile procedure she'd ever done, she thought grimly, but it couldn't be helped and infection was the least of their worries right now.

With the lines established, she let the farmer's pain relief kick in. He dozed and she no longer fought to keep him awake. Sleep was the best thing. The less stress he was under the better.

At least his head wound had ceased bleeding. She had no way of telling what the damage was to his legs. That would have to wait. Meanwhile, his pulse seemed to be getting stronger. Surely that meant there wasn't a leg wound spurting blood. Surely that meant he had a chance.

Please...

'How's it going, Dr Campbell?' If Nate hadn't been constantly there she would have gone mad, she thought, but he hardly stopped talking. He told her every single thing that was happening on the outside world. 'We have twenty men and a truckload of shoring timbers,' he said now. 'Now we're just waiting for the crane.'

'Couldn't twenty men lift a light plane?'

'Are you suggesting they stand on your roof while they do it? You'd be squashed flat. Learn patience, Dr Campbell.'

But he was more impatient than she was. And more fearful. As confident as he sounded, she could sense the fear behind his words.

And once the whole structure moved, groaning and shifting as it resettled on its fragile base. She heard Ian whimper in pain as the timber over his legs dug deeper and Nate shouted a warning.

It didn't keep moving. The iron above her nose settled from three inches above to one inch—it was pressing hard on her breast and she could no longer get out the way she'd come in. She was as trapped as Ian. It was still OK. Just.

And finally Gemma heard the yells that signified the arrival of the crane.

Even then the danger wasn't over. There was an interminable wait.

'We're attaching cables from above,' Nate told her. 'We need to secure the plane, but if we climb over the iron then we risk collapse with the extra weight. So we're swinging men out on the crane hooks to attach cables from the air.'

Finally it was done.

'It's set,' Nate told her, trying to keep his voice calm. Trying to stem the awful anxiety. 'We're taking the plane's weight now.'

The iron creaked and groaned, but almost as soon as it moved there were men shoving in shoring timbers—at the entrance, then a foot in, then two feet, three feet—moving with a speed she hadn't thought possible. They shored it up so as the iron creaked and shifted with the release of the plane's weight it didn't shift further down onto her face but onto the solid presence of the timbers.

The iron lifted. An inch. Two, then three, then…

Then Nate was crawling in beside her, before the iron was fully lifted.

She was horrified. 'Get out. Only one of us needs to be here.'

'There's no danger now. The men will haul the iron off. Put this over you.' He'd hauled in a plate of solid steel, heavy but effective. He shoved it between their heads and the roof of the cavity so that as the men worked steadily toward them from the outside they were protected from falling dust and debris.

'Don't stay…'

'I'm staying.' His arm was around her, holding her close. She was wedged tight against the farmer and Nate found Ian's hand underneath her body so that Gemma was cradled between the two men. Ian had slipped into oblivion but Nate's presence was all she needed. Nate…

'Just wait.'

She could wait. All of a sudden the fear had been lifted. All she could feel was Nate.

There was a shout of triumph and then miraculously the sheet of iron was lifted away. Instead of staring into darkness, she was staring into the sunlight and the shock was so great she closed her eyes in disbelief.

Daylight…

There were men helping her to her feet—men taking the plasma and saline bags from her—holding them up while more men worked on the timbers trapping Ian.

Nate's arm was steadying her, ensuring she was OK.

'I'm fine.' She wasn't. She was shaking like a leaf but there were more important things to worry about than her wobbly knees. 'Look after Ian.'

They were lifting the big beam holding Ian. He'd fallen

face forward and the beam was lying over his back. No
wonder he hadn't been able to move. But…it didn't look
crushed, she thought. There was debris holding either end,
so most of its weight wasn't on him.

Maybe he'd been lucky. Or…relatively lucky.

Nate was kneeling beside him. The morphine Gemma
had administered had taken hold and he was barely conscious, but he was aware of the men around him. As Nate
took his hand he even managed a feeble smile.

'It's good to see you, Doc.'

'It's good to see you, too, Ian.' Nate took a neck brace
from one of the ambulancemen and fitted it with care.
'Hold still. We'll shift you just as you are.' If there was a
compression fracture of the spine the last thing they needed
was for it to shift. 'Ian, don't move your legs or arms in
any way—let us do the moving. Don't try and help us.
Can you feel your fingers and toes?'

'I don't know…'

'OK, don't worry about it. Let's get you onto a
stretcher.'

Gemma helped, and Nate let her. OK, she was slight
but she knew what she was doing. Moving a patient with
suspected spinal injuries was a skill in itself. Nate directed
with care, until he had Ian safely onto a rigid stretcher.

'Great.'

'Do we need an air ambulance?' Gemma whispered out
of Ian's hearing. 'If there's spinal compression…'

'I've got one on standby.' He hesitated and then took a
knife from his bag and sliced off the man's boots. He's
done this before, Gemma thought. As a country GP he'd
be the one who had to cope with trauma. With the boots
discarded he put a hand on Ian's shoulder, prodding him
into wakefulness.

'Ian, can you hear me?'

'Mmm.' Ian opened his eyes. 'Yeah. You sound a long way off.'

'Can you wiggle your toes for me? Try.'

They all stared at the farmer's grubby socks as if they were the most important things in the world.

And blessedly, miraculously, they wiggled.

'That's great,' Nate said, and there was a tremor of raw emotion in his voice. They weren't looking at quadriplegia here, then. 'And your fingers?'

Once again, there was a shaky wiggle.

'Geez, my back hurts…' Ian whispered. He closed his eyes and was almost immediately asleep again.

'Let's keep the air ambulance on standby.' Nate straightened. 'We'll take him in and give him an X-ray but with luck he'll be more bruised than broken.' He nodded to the men at the ends of the stretcher. 'OK, boys, load him into the ambulance. And, Gemma…'

'I'll take your car if you want to go in the ambulance.' The local ambulance was manned by volunteers—which was why it had taken so long to get there. The ambulance officers were a plumber and a schoolteacher respectively. They had first-aid training and nothing else.

But there was no way Nate was letting Gemma drive herself—or do anything herself. 'Nope.' He threw his car keys to the fire chief. 'We both go in the ambulance,' he told her. 'And you, Dr Campbell, will go lying down.'

'No.'

'If you don't lie down you'll fall down,' he told her, and she realised suddenly that what he was saying was the truth. Reaction was setting in and her knees were threatening to give way.

'OK.' He looked down at her and he smiled—and what a smile! It was a smile she'd never seen in her life before.

'What…what?'

She was too tired, too battered to think. All she knew

was that Nate's arm was around her and she was where
she most wanted to be in the world.

'How's my patient?'

'You mean me?' Gemma woke to confusion and found
Nate smiling down at her.

'Who else would I mean?'

For a moment she was thoroughly confused. She was
lying in her gorgeous four-poster bed. Mrs McCurdle had
taken charge when she'd arrived home, clucking like a
mother hen. Then Jane had arrived. 'OK, I'm on night duty
but when something like this happens we all come in—
and there's enough staff without me sticking my oar in.'
Together they'd washed Gemma's scratches, applied
enough sticking plaster to provide a small assembly line
with a week's work and settled her under the bedcovers.

'I don't want to be here,' she'd said, distressed, and Jane
had fixed her with a look.

'Dr Ethan says if you try and move we're to sit on you.'

'I should be helping.'

'The pilot's dead,' Jane had told her bluntly. 'He's beyond help. And Ian's being taken through to X-ray right
now. If Dr Ethan needs you then he'll call, but for the
moment we're under instructions to keep you where you
are.'

So Gemma lay and fretted, wanting to get up but aware
at the same time that she was trembling all over. Mrs
McCurdle provided hot tea and hot-water bottles but
Gemma still couldn't get warm.

And then Nate arrived, crossing swiftly to the bed, and
her heart started hammering even harder than it had when
she'd thought she might die.

'Gemma...' There was such tenderness in his voice that
it made her blink. He sounded...different.

'How goes it?' Why wouldn't her voice work properly? She tried again. 'Ian...'

'Ian is going to be OK. He's one very lucky farmer.' Nate sank onto her bed and lifted her hand, linking her fingers with his. It was a gesture of comfort, she told herself. Nothing more. So there was no reason at all for her heart to hammer even harder. 'The X-rays show a greenstick fracture of his forearm and a couple of broken ribs. That's all. His spine is only bruised—the numbness was temporary, caused by the blow, and now it's completely gone. That's not to say he won't be sorry for himself for a good long while—that was a huge beam that slammed down on him. Graham and I have stitched his head, strapped his ribs and set his fracture and now he's fast asleep. Like you should be.'

'I'm not sleepy.'

He smiled down at her, with that smile that had her heart doing somersaults. 'How about if I give you something to make you sleep?'

'No. I should get up. Cady...'

'Milly's mother collected Cady an hour ago and has taken him out to have a party tea.'

'Wh-why?'

'Because she heard what was happening, of course. That's what country practice is all about, Gemma. People looking after their own.'

And still his hand held hers. *People looking after their own.* That was how she felt, she thought, and it was the strangest sensation. Like she was cherished.

People didn't cherish the likes of Gemma Campbell.

'You realise you saved Ian's life?'

'I didn't—'

'He'd have bled to death in there, Gemma. You risked your life to save him. In fact, you risked your life to save us. Going near that damned power pole... And the community knows it. Ian's wife is with him now. She'd normally have been in the dairy with him but she'd taken the kids to the city, shopping, so there's another little miracle for you. She's ready to fall on your chest with gratitude.'

'I don't—'

'You don't think you're up to having anyone falling on your chest?'

'Um, no,' she managed, and he chuckled.

'Jane says a couple of your scratches are deep. Can I see?'

'No.'

'I'm a doctor.'

'Yeah, and so am I,' she said with a note of asperity. 'I can check my own scratches, thank you very much.' The scratches Jane was talking about were in places she wasn't having this man look at in a million years.

'You're sure?'

'I'm sure.'

'Gemma…'

'Mmm.' She was still defensive. Still trying desperately to maintain an armour plating round her heart. What was it with this man? He just had to look at her and she felt like jelly.

'Gemma, when that iron shifted…when you were underneath…'

'It wasn't a good moment,' she admitted, and Nate closed his eyes.

'No, Gemma. It wasn't a good moment. It made me see…' Nate hesitated, and the grip on her hand tightened. He opened his eyes but he wasn't looking at her. It was as if he was looking into an abyss. 'It made me see how much…how much you're starting to mean to me.'

'I don't—'

'No, let me finish.' He did look at her then, his dark

eyes meeting hers and holding her gaze. 'When I asked you to marry me…I was stupid.'

'Well, there's one thing we agree on,' she whispered, but he shook his head.

'No. I wasn't stupid for asking you to marry me. In fact, I've never done anything so sensible in my life. But I was stupid when I thought that we could lead separate, independent lives.'

'Nate—'

'No, let me finish.' He'd been shaken to the core. There was emotion in his voice—Nate Ethan had been thrown right off track and he was trying to make sense of it. 'My parents didn't have a good marriage. They had…well, I guess it could be called a marriage of convenience. My mother was a society hostess and my father was a brilliant surgeon. The role model they gave me was a marriage where the partners only came together as a matter of convenience. And I thought, well, for a long time that was what I thought should happen to me. Sure the life they led left me cold—that was why I turned to country medicine. But as for contact…as for loving…'

'Nate, you're shaken up.' Somehow Gemma managed to make sense of this. Somehow. 'You've had a shock. You've had two weeks of shocks. You learned that you have a baby. You've seen a man killed and you've been traumatised by this afternoon's events. Now's not the time to be saying—'

'Now *is* the time to be saying. Marriage as a convenience… I must have been mad. It was only because I hadn't yet met the right woman. And now I have. Hell, Gemma, I think I'm in love with you.'

There. The thing was said and it was out in the open.

He couldn't believe he'd said it.

He looked…astonished, Gemma thought. As if he didn't believe he was capable of such a thing.

He loved her?

People didn't love Gemma Campbell.

'Nate, you've had a fright,' she said wearily. 'You'll see things differently in the morning.'

'I won't.'

She shrugged. There was a tiny part of her—a small warm core of her—that wanted to say yes! That wanted to accept every protestation this man could make. That wanted to take his face between her scratched hands and kiss him and kiss him...

To make him hers.

What was she thinking of? She wasn't free to love this man. She couldn't take him even if she wanted him.

'Gemma...' His hands were on her face, forcing her eyes to meet his. A girl could drown in those eyes, she thought drearily. If she could just let herself...

No. She'd let him kiss her once and that way could only lead to disaster. Somehow she had to pull back—to make him see.

'Nate, I don't want this.'

'You do.'

'No.'

'Why not? It could be so great. You and me...'

'No!'

'You're tired.' His eyes were searching hers, puzzled and concerned. He didn't understand. Well, why should he? She barely understood herself.

She was tired. Right, that was it. She was tired. 'Yes.' It sounded pathetic. *She* sounded pathetic.

'We'll talk in the morning.'

'Yes.' Maybe in the morning she'd have herself together. She'd have her armour back in place.

But she so wanted to kiss him.

'You'd better go...'

'Mmm.' But he didn't. His hands were still holding her

face. He gazed down at her for a long, long minute and then very slowly he lowered his mouth onto hers.

She should refuse. She should push him away—shove—do anything but let herself sink into that kiss.

But she was no longer capable of fighting. She was no longer capable of pushing him away. Because suddenly there was nothing in this world except Nate. Nate holding her, Nate's eyes searching hers, Nate's mouth pressing against hers... Her brain told her to push this man away but her brain wasn't the major force any more.

So what was? She didn't know. All she knew was that it was a force as strong as life itself. Man meeting woman and merging with passion and with love. She wanted to push him away but her arms wouldn't work. Nothing worked. Only the need of him—the want.

The love.

She gave a tiny moan and tried again to break away but it must have felt like encouragement to the man who'd gathered her in his arms. He was deepening the kiss. Searching her mouth. Searching her soul...

He felt so good. So right. The only thing in her world was Nate. His hands, his mouth and his body.

Nate.

Her body was aching for him. Her lips—her breasts—her thighs. In his arms the dangers of the day faded to nothing. Here was her life. Here was her home.

He'd said he loved her!

She should fight but was no longer capable of fighting. For this one wonderful interlude she abandoned herself to his kiss. Glorying in the fact that she could be loved. She, Gemma...

There was a knock on the door.

Hell!

They pulled apart. Somehow they pulled apart—just.

Inches only. Gemma looked up at the man beside her, and her face was dazed with confusion.

And Nate's expression mirrored hers.

But the knocking continued. 'Yes?' Nate's voice was distant, as if the outside world had nothing to do with what was happening here.

But the outside world was intent on intrusion. Jane was peering around the door and her expression was rueful. It was as if she knew what she'd interrupted and she hated doing it.

'Gemma?'

'Mmm.' Gemma was still looking at Nate.

'There's a man outside who wants to see you,' she said, and her voice was tinged with uncertainty. 'Gemma, he says he's your husband.'

CHAPTER NINE

WHAT the hell…?

Nate made his way back to the wards, his head spinning. He'd only had a glimpse of the man waiting to see Gemma—a big man in his early thirties, smoothly dressed and immaculately groomed. He was wearing a three-piece suit, Italian cut and expensive. Nate hadn't liked what he'd seen—but he wasn't in the mood for liking.

Gemma's husband.

She hadn't said she was still married.

Or had she?

Maybe he'd just assumed it was over. He'd never thought there could possibly be a man in the wings waiting to claim her.

'Is something wrong?' He started as Graham's hand came down on his shoulder and he wheeled to face the older man. He didn't want to face anyone—especially not someone whose eyes saw as much as Graham's did.

'No.'

But Graham did see. Sort of. He knew enough to sense that something was troubling Nate. Something more than the tragedy of the afternoon. And what he had to ask wouldn't make things easier. 'They've brought the pilot in. You want to get this over with?'

Great. A post-mortem. Just what he needed to finish off a perfect day.

'Hell.'

'I can do it myself.'

He collected himself at that. Post-mortems in this community were the devil. Everyone knew everyone—there was no such thing as an autopsy on a stranger.

'If you're really cut up we could send him to Blairglen,' Graham suggested. 'But Olive...'

Hector's wife. Olive.

'She'd like him to stay here,' Graham said softly. He was watching Nate's face, trying to figure out what was troubling him. Was it this useless death—or something more?

Something more, he decided. Gemma?

'Let's do it,' Nate snapped before Graham could think further. 'Hell. I don't want to do this.'

'Neither do I.'

'Then let's get it over with.'

The post-mortem was bad enough. The interview with Olive afterwards was worse.

'The fool.' She was so angry she was nearly spitting. Grief would come later, Nate knew, but for now all she could see was the waste. 'That damned boundary dispute. It consumed him. They said he was trying to spook Ian's cows when he flew into power lines. The fool. Oh, the damned fool...'

'He died instantly,' Nate told her, knowing that she'd hear and that later it would provide a modicum of comfort.

'You think I care?'

'I think you care,' he said gently, and propelled her into a chair.

'The damned feud...and he's left me for it.'

'I'm sure he didn't mean—'

'He didn't mean to kill himself, but he meant nothing but mischief. And I loved him.' She raised tear-drenched eyes to Nate and gulped back a body-wrenching sob. 'I loved him. What am I going to do now?'

*   *   *

And that was the whole trouble, Nate thought as he caught up with the medical needs of the little community—the firefighter who'd ripped his leg on a piece of roofing iron, the dead pilot's mother needing tranquillisers to get her through the first awful spasm of grief, Ian needing more painkillers and reassurance, and his wife and children to counsel.

The phrase kept running over and over in his head. *I loved him. What am I going to do now?*

He changed the one word.

I loved her. What am I going to do now?

Then he realised he had the tense wrong.

I love her.

How had he got himself into this mess? He'd never planned to fall in love. He didn't know how on earth it had happened.

At nine o'clock Sandra Jefferson returned with a very sleepy—and very contented—Cady. 'They've had a wonderful time,' she told him. 'Any time you want Cady looked after, feel free to call on me. He and Milly get on so well—it's just lovely.'

It was lovely.

What would happen now? Nate wondered as he took Cady's sugar levels and gave him his nightly dose of insulin. He really was the best kid—he didn't protest at all. He'd adjusted very easily to his new regime.

The thought of losing him was almost as wrenching as the thought of losing Gemma.

Hell, what was happening to him? Had he fallen for Cady as well as Gemma? What was it?

Why should he care?

But he did. Would Cady return to the city? And what on earth was happening with Gemma? Why had she decided to stay in the first place if she had a husband?

With Cady snuggled up fast asleep, Nate checked his

daughter and found she was also sleeping and then he thought, What now? Should he go back to Gemma's bedroom?

No. Because how on earth could he look at her without emotion threatening to overwhelm him?

Graham came into the kitchen and his face was impassive.

'There's a bloke out there wants to see you.'

'Yeah?'

'I've put him in your waiting room. You want me to come with you?'

'Why would you want to do that?'

'He says he's Cady's father.'

Silence. Then... 'Cady's father,' Nate said cautiously. 'You're kidding.'

'That's what he says'

'Big bloke? Expensive suit?'

'That's the one.'

'But I thought...'

'You thought what?'

'If he's the man who was here earlier, he said that he's Gemma's husband.'

'So?' Then Graham thought it through and saw what Nate was confused about. 'But Cady is Fiona's kid.'

'Yeah.'

'Then Cady can't be Gemma's husband's kid? Can he? Am I missing something here?'

Nate shook his head. 'Not that I can see. I'm as confused as you are.'

'The plot gets more convoluted by the minute.' Graham looked bemused. And also concerned. 'I suppose the man could have formally adopted Cady. He might have if he was...if he *is* married to Gemma.'

First impressions were often correct and this one was spot on. Nate had looked at the man as he'd waited outside

Gemma's room and he hadn't liked what he'd seen and he didn't like what he saw when he walked back into his waiting room.

'You wanted to see me?'

'You're Nate Ethan?'

'Yes.'

'And you're looking after my wife and my kid?'

Gemma and Cady.

'Yes.'

'Then I'm here to tell you that I'm taking them back to Sydney. Tomorrow.'

'Do they want to go back to Sydney?' Somehow Nate kept his voice neutral—calm in the face of belligerence.

'Of course they want to come.'

'I'm sorry but they've been here for two weeks and you've hardly been mentioned.'

'But I have been mentioned.'

He couldn't deny it. 'Yes.'

'Well, there you go, then. They've had their little holiday. Now it's time to get back to work.'

Nate hesitated, not sure where to take it. He didn't like what was happening—and he didn't understand.

'Did Gemma tell you that Cady's been diagnosed as a diabetic?'

'Yeah. That's got nothing to do with me. It's her business.'

'He needs constant medical supervision.'

'He goes to a hospital crèche. He'll get supervision there.'

'But Gemma's lost her job at the hospital.'

'She'll get another job,' he said easily, with the assurance of someone who knew they were right. 'She's an anaesthetist. They're in demand.'

The man sounded placid about it and things were sounding more and more out of kilter.

'I need to speak to Gemma,' Nate started, but the man shook his head.

'There's no need. Cady's mine—not Gemma's. She had no business bringing him down here so I'm taking him back tomorrow. If Gemma doesn't want to come with me then she can follow. But she will. Have the boy ready for me by nine.'

And that was that. He walked out and slammed the door behind him.

Cady's mine—not Gemma's.

This whole set-up wasn't making sense. Nate took a few deep breaths, went and checked on Ian just to give himself time to collect his wits—it didn't work—and finally returned to Gemma's room. She didn't look at him as he entered. She was lying flat on her pillows with her arms behind her head and her face set like stone.

The impulse was to walk straight over and take her in his arms, but there was something about that expression... It was a shield all by itself.

'Gemma...'

'I'm sorry,' she said blankly. 'Nate, I'm sorry.'

'Do you want to tell me what you're sorry about?'

'I thought...I thought he mightn't want us. I was stupid.' Still she wouldn't look at him. It was as if she was afraid of what she might see.

Nate hesitated and then sat down on the bed beside her. He tried to take her hand but she pulled away. Keeping up the shield. 'Do you want to tell me about it?'

'No.'

'I'm a good listener.'

'And I married Alan. End of story.' She flung the words at him like a taunt. 'I never should have... I never dreamed it was possible. You and me. Staying here. It was a crazy idea, doomed from the start.'

'Because you're married?'

'Because I was married.'

'Right.' He nodded as if he understood everything. Which he didn't. 'Um... You and...'

'Alan. His name's Alan Herbert.'

'Right. But you're not Mrs Herbert?'

'I kept my maiden name—for my medicine. And afterwards...'

'Afterwards?'

'After we divorced.'

Divorced. That had a good ring to it. Divorced was something at least. But he still didn't understand. 'I got the impression,' Nate said cautiously, 'that you hadn't divorced. That you're returning to Sydney with him in the morning.'

'He said that?'

'It's not true?' There was a flicker of hope in his voice, quashed immediately by the shake of her head.

'Oh, it's true all right.'

'You're not still in love with him?'

'Are you kidding?' But her voice sounded dead. Like all the life had been sucked out of it. 'After what he did...'

'Gemma, you're going to have to tell me.'

'You don't want to know.'

'Try me.'

She shook her head. Still she refused to look at him. 'Leave it, Nate.'

'Is Alan Cady's father?'

She drew in her breath. 'Yes.'

'But Cady is your sister's son.'

'That's the one.'

'So Fiona and Alan...'

'Didn't I tell you?' she demanded bleakly. 'Didn't I

make you see? Everything I had, Fiona wanted, and she was like that from the time that I can first remember. My toys, my clothes, my mother's attention. Then my career—and my husband.'

'So she and Alan...'

'Alan was a dreadful choice for a husband,' she said bitterly. 'He's an accountant at Sydney Central. He took me out a couple of times but it was my earning capacity he was interested in. Not me. Only I was too stupid to see it. Then he met Fiona. Well, that was that. He was obsessed, but he was careful. Incredibly careful. Fiona didn't want anything to do with him, and he hid his obsession well. He became...loving. And I fell for it. I married him.'

'Which was a nightmare?'

'Of course it was a nightmare.' Her voice was devoid of emotion. Deadpan. It was like she was recounting the story of someone she hardly knew. 'Alan seemed to understand Fiona. Somehow he knew the only way she'd be interested in him was if I loved him. And there was still the fact that I was a good meal ticket. Anaesthetics is one of the best-paid medical specialties in the country, and greed is Alan's middle name. Those two reasons, greed and Fiona, were why he married me.' She gave a harsh laugh that was totally devoid of humour. 'Well, why else? Why else would anyone want the likes of me?'

'Gemma...'

'Let me finish,' she said bleakly. 'You might as well know the whole sordid business.'

'Not if it hurts.'

'It doesn't hurt.' And then she shrugged. 'Who am I kidding? Of course it hurts. It hurts mostly because I was so stupid.'

'Alan and Fiona...'

'Were an item almost as soon as we were married,' Gemma told him. 'Alan's reasoning paid off. Fiona wasn't

interested in Alan the accountant. But Alan my husband…
That was a different story. Almost as soon as I realised
why he'd married me, Fiona took what she wanted. When
she was pregnant with Cady she threw it in my face. Once
more Fiona triumphed. Once more…'

Nate took a deep breath, hearing the depth of pain in
Gemma's voice. 'And…'

'I left Alan, of course, and Alan moved in with Fiona.
He had what he wanted. Or he thought he did. But Cady
was born, and caring for a baby didn't fit either of their
lifestyles, and, of course, Fiona didn't really want Alan.
After she'd proved she could have him, the fun had gone
out of it. Alan was left angry and bitter, reflecting that
he'd lost not only Fiona but my lucrative salary. Which he
really wanted. And then there was Cady, caught between
parents who didn't give a damn. Fiona knew I'd step in—
all she had to do was neglect him and in I'd come. Which
I did. But instead of only Fiona using me, now there was
Alan.'

'I don't see…'

'He's Cady's father. He has rights that as his aunt I don't
have.'

'So…'

'Alan might be a successful accountant but he has expensive tastes. Very expensive tastes. And he's given me
an ultimatum. I continue working as an anaesthetist, giving
more than half of my income to him, or he'll take Cady
back. It's not even a choice. It's a life sentence.'

Nate was staring at her in revulsion. 'Does he love
Cady?'

'You have to be joking! Love? I don't think Alan knows
what the word means.'

Nate stared down at her in horror, appalled by what he'd
just been told. 'You should have told me.'

'Yeah, right. This is a sordid little mess that only I can

get out of. I thought… Well, since Fiona died I haven't heard from him. I hoped—desperately—that he'd decided to leave us alone. So when you offered me the job here I thought, Well, why not? A new life. A new beginning. But, of course, he'd know where I was. He works in Administration at Sydney Central. He'd have known that I'd left, and a quick search of medical records would have told him that I've been practising here. So here he is, right on cue, ready to hound me back to practising as an anaesthetist. Alan will never be content with what I earn as a country doctor.'

Nate took a deep breath, trying to take it all in. 'So…'

'So I go back to the city and get another high-earning job or he'll take Cady away from me.'

'He doesn't want Cady. That much is obvious. He might take him but the novelty would soon wear off…'

'Leaving me to pick up the pieces. Great. You must see as clearly as I do that I can't take that risk.'

'So where does that leave…us?'

Gemma stirred then and for the first time she turned in her bed to look at Nate. Really look at him. Behind her eyes was a desolation that chilled him to the bone.

'Nate, there is no us.'

'There must be.'

'No. Tomorrow I pack my bags and head back to Sydney. I love Cady and I'll do everything in my power to keep him safe.'

'Gemma, you can't keep on paying for ever.'

'I don't need to. In another five or six years—if Cady's been living with me full time—then I might have grounds to be appointed his guardian. But now…if there was legal argument then Alan would win.'

'You know that for sure?'

'I'm not a fool. I've paid for legal advice. Alan is his biological father and I… I'm just his aunt. His aunt who loves him but his aunt nonetheless. Alan has the resources to care for a child and he has the money to fight for him. Cady's birth certificate has him named as Cady's father. Alan was living with Fiona when he was born. So you see? There's no contest.'

'Hell.'

'It is hell,' she whispered. 'But, Nate…'

'Yes?'

'Thank you for the last two weeks. They've been wonderful.'

They had, he thought bleakly. They had.

Suddenly he realised just how wonderful.

She'd changed him, he thought. In a brief two weeks he'd been taught to care for something other than himself. Oh, sure, he loved Graham and he cared deeply about his patients but it wasn't like this. This need to lift the burdens of the world from Gemma's shoulders. To take her and love her and set her world to rights.

Knowing he couldn't.

'I'll ring Mike,' he said harshly. 'My lawyer friend in Sydney. He's the one who advised me about Margot.'

Margot. Right. Her ex-boss. The Margot of a world away.

'There's nothing you can do,' Gemma told him. 'Believe me, I've paid for the best legal advice. They played happy families and that closed every legal loophole for me. Fiona and Alan, with Cady in the middle. Cady who didn't get a look in because they were too busy playing games. Fiona never wanted Cady. She didn't even want Alan. She just wanted to hurt me.'

'And Alan?'

'Alan just wants money.' She shook her head. 'I was too stupid to see. I've always been so alone. When I met Alan… I had my head in my books trying to pass exams so that I could be an anaesthetist, and Alan was so courteous and charming. He made me laugh. He made me think he cared. But, of course, he just wanted a wife who was going to add to his bank balance.'

'You can't go back to him!'

'Of course I can't. Even if I did that's not what Alan wants. He just wants my paycheque.'

'It's blackmail.'

'Yes, but it's a very effective form of blackmail. I won't let Cady go back to him.'

'So call his bluff.'

'He'll take him. You don't know Alan. He's smooth and clever and nasty. He'll take Cady—he's done it once before. Cady was looked after physically. There were no grounds to report him to welfare. No grounds for me to take him away. But Cady...well, he's not going back there even if I have to pay for the rest of my life.'

'So where does that leave you and me?'

'You and me were a dream.' Gemma closed her eyes and there was such pain in her voice that Nate couldn't bear it. He caught her hands and held them, willing warmth into their chill. Willing love...

'I'll kill the bastard...'

'Oh, right. That'd help.' She gave a laugh that was half a sob.

'Gemma, this is impossible. Let me talk to him. Maybe we—'

'Maybe we nothing.' She took a deep breath. 'There is no we, Nate. This is my problem. Mine. I came down here to give you your daughter. I've done that. And I know you'll love her. You don't know how much that means to me.'

'I can guess.'

'Nate...' She shook her head—a desolate little gesture that made him want to wrap her in his arms and hold her.

But when he moved toward her she shrank back against the pillows.

'No, Nate, I can't.'

'You can't...what?'

'I can't go any further with you. I'm leaving here in the morning. Me and Cady. We've done what we set out to do. You've given us—me and Cady—two weeks which we'll remember for the rest of our lives. And that's it.'

'It's not it.'

'There's nothing else to do about it.'

'Maybe there is,' he growled. He stared at her in baffled anger, his frustration growing by the moment.

'There isn't.'

'There is,' he said savagely. 'I just haven't thought what it is yet.'

CHAPTER TEN

IT WAS a tough night for sleeping.

It was a tough night for doing anything at all. Gemma lay awake and stared into the darkness and she'd never felt so bleak in all her life.

This had been a dream. These two weeks…

A dream was how she'd have to remember it, she decided. A wonderful, magical fantasy where people cared and Cady was happy and loved and she…

And she herself was loved.

So of course it was a dream. People didn't love Gemma. Had she learned nothing over the years?

Nate loved her.

No, she corrected herself. Nate felt sorry for her. She'd leave and he'd go back to Donna or someone like her.

But it had felt so right. So wonderfully right. Like two halves of a whole, they fitted together. Man and woman.

They didn't fit together any more. As of tomorrow she'd be gone. Back to the city to find another high-powered job to keep Alan happy. To keep Cady safe.

But at such a cost?

'You're letting her go?'

'What else can I do?' Nate had explained the situation to his uncle and Graham was as appalled as he was.

'I don't know. Pistols at dawn seems a good option. With only one pistol loaded.'

'I won't be much good to Gemma in jail.'

'And he's definitely the boy's father? He does have legal rights?'

171

'You know the custody laws. Unless there are exceptional circumstances, the natural parents will always win. Gemma's had legal advice. She's stuck.'

'We can't pay him off?'

'Are you kidding?' Nate looked at his uncle with affectionate exasperation. 'With what? Hell, the one thing we don't do here is make money. We might—if you ever agreed to charge people what you're worth.'

Graham bristled. 'I suppose you do? What about the time you spent with Olive today? I'll bet that's not been charged. You might charge Ian for the time you spent sewing him up, but did you charge for the hours you spent in the paddock? I don't think so. Country doctors don't make any money, boy. Not if they have hearts.'

That was just the trouble. Nate had a brief flash of what could be—him moving to the city—making megabucks—getting rid of Alan—but that was all it was. A brief flash of hopeless imagining.

He'd come down here six years ago to help Graham out, and his heart had been well and truly caught. Now being a country doctor was who he was. It was his identity. Surgical practice in the city would mean walking away from Graham—and, more, walking away from a community who depended on him. He knew what the odds were of finding someone to take his place.

Doctors didn't like moving to the country.

He stared bleakly across the table at Graham and thought, I'm as trapped as Gemma.

'I suppose he really is the boy's father?' Graham was still thinking things through.

'Fiona put him down on the birth certificate. Just like she named me. There's no possibility that I'm not Mia's father.'

'You can't fight that one. Not with that hair. So…does Cady look like this guy?'

'I guess.' He frowned. 'A bit. But there doesn't seem to be any doubt. Gemma said they were even living together for a while. What the pair of them wouldn't do to hurt her...'

'That's what I mean.' Graham shook his head. 'It's a long shot—but I guess it's a stupid suggestion. Whoever the father is, it's definitely not you. Which is all that matters.'

'Hell, I wish I was.'

'Do you really?' Graham asked curiously. 'Two weeks ago the thought of marriage was giving you the collywobbles. Now you have a daughter. Do you want a son as well?'

There was no hesitation. 'Yes. And a wife.' He groaned and slammed his fist down on the table so hard that it hurt. 'More than anything else in the world.'

Nate lay awake far into the night, his trapped mind examining every possibility he could think of. Twisting this way and that. Trying to see a way out of this mess.

And at three in the morning he sat up and turned the light on. A conversation was playing over and over in his head.

It was his brief conversation with Jeff, his pathologist friend from Sydney Central, when he'd been checking on Gemma's credentials. He hadn't understood the conversation then and he didn't understand it now.

What had he said?

He got up and made himself a cup of coffee, thinking back to the conversation. He'd thought it odd at the time, which was why he remembered it

Did he have it right?

'Margot couldn't stand the sister. Come to think of it, no one could—once you got to see past that beautiful face.

She was as mad as a cut snake and what she and that husband of hers did to Gemma...'

And...

'They fed her a pack of lies. And she believed it. Hell, as far as I know, she still believes it. She won't talk about Fiona to anyone.'

Hell.

He let his coffee get cold and paced a bit while he thought about it some more.

It was a long shot—a crazy shot.

He'd never get anything out of Jeff.

Would he?

Damn, it was three in the morning.

No matter. He picked up the phone and dialled Sydney Central.

'Can you put me through to Jeff Sandhurst, please? Yes, I realise he's not on duty and I know it's three in the morning. Yes, I realise... But it's urgent. Tell him it's Dr Nate Ethan from Terama and I need to speak to him— *now.'*

CHAPTER ELEVEN

NATE rose before dawn. Well, he couldn't sleep so he decided he might as well work.

First there was a letter to write. A letter that was short and to the point and entirely satisfactory. He hoped.

Then he did some random medico-legal paperwork while he waited for his patients to wake, then spent much longer than usual visiting each of them. He was killing time. He wasn't facing Gemma with what he'd found out. Or what he planned. Who knew how she'd react? And this was too important for her to have scruples.

This wasn't pistols at dawn but it was just as unethical.

Nine o'clock seemed a long way off.

His last patient was the farmer they'd pulled from under the plane, and Ian wasn't impressed by the dark shadows under his eyes.

'Hell, Doc, you look as bad as me.' Ian was recovering beautifully. He was tackling his breakfast bacon and eggs with all the trimmings which, considering the condition he'd been in the night before, was little short of a miracle. 'Did you have trouble during the night?'

'Um...yes.' It seemed safer to agree.

'Not as dramatic as our accident, I hope.' Ian's face became closed and he winced as he shifted against the pillows. He wasn't quite as great as he made out. 'Of all the stupid accidents. I've been thinking and thinking. I should have let him have his four feet of land. It was a strip four feet wide and fifty feet long. That's the strip we were fighting over. And he died for it.'

'I'm sorry.'

'Maybe we just had to fight.' Ian shook his head. 'Maybe we even enjoyed the drama of the thing. Seems we've been shouting over the fence at each other since we were lads.' His weathered face puckered in distress. 'Hell. The whole thing seems so damned pointless now. How's Olive?'

'Terrible.' There was no point in dissembling.

'Tell her I'll milk her cows. I'm mostly running beef cattle now and I've only got forty milkers. I can easily run her herd with ours. We'll split the milk income and it won't cost her a thing.'

And why couldn't he have been as accommodating as this before Hector killed himself? Nate wondered. Why on earth did people fight?

Why had Fiona wanted to hurt Gemma so badly?

Maybe she'd sensed that it hadn't only been in health that Gemma had surpassed her, he thought. She'd been jealous of Gemma long before she'd been diagnosed with diabetes.

Maybe it was because Gemma was just…good.

What would Gemma say if she knew what he was about to do?

He wouldn't tell her. He'd stay away from her until it was time.

'What the mind doesn't know the heart doesn't grieve over,' he said to himself—and then he thought, Heck, the medical board could come down on him like a ton of bricks…if Alan called his bluff… He who dares wins.

'And if I mouth one more platitude I'm going to go out of my mind,' he told himself grimly. 'Bring on nine o'clock.'

At nine Gemma was packed and ready to go. Cady had his own little suitcase packed. He was tearful, clinging to Mrs McCurdle as if he was being torn apart.

Gemma wasn't tearful. She was just…blank.

'You don't need to say goodbye,' she told Nate when he finally left his patients and came to find her. She was standing on the veranda, waiting. Alan had told her that he was driving Cady back to Sydney and she was to follow in her own car.

With Cady on board he was sure she'd follow.

'I'm staying,' Nate told her. He was standing on the veranda with his daughter cradled in his arms. Mia was fast asleep but for some reason Nate had fetched her from her cot. It was as if he wanted Mia to say her own good-bye.

Graham had said goodbye briefly—harshly. There'd been raw emotion in the old man's voice as he'd escaped to the surgery, leaving Nate to see them off.

So the scene was set. Nate looked across at Cady and he hesitated. The little boy was too dark. Too like his mother.

He'd be better off away from the veranda where Alan couldn't see him.

'You haven't said goodbye to Rufus,' he told the boy, touching him lightly on his shoulder and sending an urgent message to Mrs McCurdle with his eyes. 'Helen, what about taking Cady into the kitchen and bringing him back out when Alan gets here?'

'I don't like my daddy,' Cady sobbed, and Mrs McCurdle hiccuped on her own sob and took him back into the house.

Which left Nate and Gemma. And Mia.

'I don't know how to thank you,' Gemma started, but he shook his head and looked down at the sleeping Mia.

'There's no need. You've given me my daughter. It's me who owes you. But there's something I want you to do for me.'

'What?'

'When Alan comes…I want you to shut up and listen.'

She frowned in incomprehension. 'Why?'

'Just… Whatever I say, you're not to contradict me. Do you hear?'

'I…' She still didn't understand but his eyes were compelling. She shrugged. 'OK. I guess.'

'Then let's just put these suitcases back inside in the hall,' he suggested, heaving them back inside the door and out of the way. 'Just in case they're not wanted.'

Alan arrived just when he'd said he would. He was driving a Porsche, and Nate looked from the gleaming car to Gemma's battered old Datsun and any last qualms he had about what he was doing faded to nothing. By the time Alan climbed from his car Nate was ready—with words if not with pistols.

And a letter…

'Is the boy ready?' Alan didn't bother with greetings. He was focused on Gemma and his dislike was obvious. Whatever pretence he'd ever made of loving this woman was long gone. She was now only a tool.

Gemma's face was pure misery. So much so that Nate felt like going in boots and all.

Which would have been stupid.

'He's…he's in the kitchen, saying goodbye to the dog,' Gemma faltered, trying not to look at Nate. 'I'll go and fetch him.'

'Don't fetch him yet, Gem.' Nate's voice was soft and dangerous. He was calmly watchful and his eyes didn't leave Alan's face. 'There's a few things I want to have out with Alan first.'

'Like what?' Alan already had his hand on the screen door. 'I don't have time to mess around. I've wasted enough time already.'

Nate chose his words with care.

'Then I'll be blunt. If you're thinking of taking *my son* back to Sydney, it's time you thought again.'

'*My son.*'

The words spun around them. Alan stopped dead and stared.

Nate stood calmly unconcerned, cradling his daughter as if he hadn't just dropped a bombshell. He'd let the blanket fall away so Mia's red hair—Nate's red hair—was clearly visible.

'I don't want your kid,' Alan said at last, regaining his composure after what he obviously thought was a mistake. 'I want mine.'

'But I'm not talking about my daughter.' Nate's tone was still steady. Alan clearly hadn't taken it on board that Mia was a girl. 'I'm talking about my son.'

Alan stared. 'You mean…Cady?'

'I mean Cady.'

Silence. Gemma didn't say a word. How could she? She was so stunned she was having trouble standing up. She reached out and grabbed a veranda rail and held on as if she needed support.

She did.

'I don't know what the hell you're talking about,' Alan said at last, and hauled the screen door open—but Nate's voice cut like a whip.

'I think you do. I think you know very well that Cady is my son. Not yours.'

'He's not—'

'I fathered two children for Fiona,' Nate went on ruthlessly. 'She used me—she chose me and she used me but I let myself be used. Well, why not? If it wasn't me then it would have been someone else, and she promised that I wouldn't be liable for their care. But she left me in no doubt that I was the father.'

'I don't... This is nonsense...'

'Do you want to see the letter she wrote to me after Cady was born?' Nate shoved his free hand in his pocket and brought out a typed note. It looked battered and frayed around the edges as if it had been read and reread a hundred times. 'Let me read it to you.'

And because there was no reply—there could be no reply when both were stunned into silence—he read aloud.

'Dear Nate,

'I thought you should know that you have a son. I've called him Cady. Cute, huh? As I told you, there's no problem with paternity—I've suckered my sister's husband into thinking he's the father. He has far more resources than you to finance the kid's upkeep, and this'll pay off a few scores to my sister as well. But I thought you should know your genes live on. And who knows...if I want another kid some day I know where to find you. The sex was great.
'Fiona'

Silence, silence and more silence. It stretched on and on into infinity.

'I always thought the boy would be OK,' Nate said at last. 'I thought he'd be looked after. And let's face it, fatherhood wasn't my style—though the thought of planting a few genes in a woman as gorgeous as Fiona had definite appeal. So I thought no more of it. After this note I didn't hear from her for three years. Until she wanted another baby.'

He proffered Mia to Alan—who almost flinched. Nate smiled. 'Then—after I fathered Mia—I heard nothing again. Nor did I expect to. It was a hell of a shock when Gemma brought me my daughter, told me Fiona was dead

MARION LENNOX   181

and I found out what sort of scumbag was playing father to my son.'

'You don't... You can't...'

'Can't what?'

'Cady is...'

'Are you denying the children are mine?' Nate lifted the blanket right away from Mia's face then, so her colouring was clear to all of them. The similarities were striking. 'You *are* kidding.'

'Cady...'

'Cady's colouring's not as obvious,' Nate told him. 'But the similarities are there.'

'I don't believe you.'

'Then let's do a blood test, shall we?' Nate said softly—and watched Alan's face lose its colour. 'A DNA test can be done very easily. It'll establish once and for all that I fathered both the children.'

He was mad, Gemma thought blindly. Stark staring mad!

Alan was staring at Nate with such vicious hatred in his eyes that Gemma felt sick. If there'd been pistols available there'd have been blood spilt, she thought.

There was a baby between them.

Nate's smile was polite and cold and absolutely implacable.

'Get your butt off my property,' he told him.

'You—'

'Now.'

To Gemma's absolute bewilderment, Alan swore once, turned on his heel—and went.

Gemma sat down—hard—right on the top step and stuck her head between her knees. By the time she raised her head the Porsche was disappearing with a screech of burned rubber and Nate was sitting down beside her. Mia slept on regardless. He held her easily in the crook of one arm—a contented dad, supremely pleased with himself

Smoking pistols wouldn't have felt half as good.

'Good, huh?' He looked modestly down at the letter in his hand and Gemma could only stare at him in disbelief.

'Fiona never wrote that letter.'

'Of course she didn't. I wrote it this morning.' His voice was smugness personified. 'Do you like the bit about the sex?'

'You…you…'

'Wonderful person?' he suggested hopefully, and she choked.

'No.'

'No?'

'No! Nate, it's not the truth.'

'It's no less of a fabrication than the lies your sister and your ex-husband have been feeding you.'

Silence. Then… 'If someone doesn't tell me what's going on,' she said softly, 'I'm going to drum my heels on the veranda and have hysterics. At full throttle.'

'Can I watch?'

'Nate…'

'Gemma.'

'Just tell me.'

'You can't guess?'

She took a deep breath. 'Somehow… Am I missing something or has Alan just conceded that he's not Cady's father?'

'I believe he's conceded that. Yes.'

'But…you're not?'

'I'm not.' He smiled, his very nicest smile that threw her into even greater turmoil than she was already feeling. 'No, Gemma. Contrary to what I told Alan, I would never knowingly agree to father a child I didn't intend to care for. I met Fiona for the first time twelve months before Mia was born.'

She thought that over and came to the obvious conclusion. 'So you lied.'

'I lied.' His virtuous look came back. 'But for a very good cause.'

'But... How did you know...how did you guess?'

'Now, that's a bit of a problem,' he told her. 'I sort of hoped you wouldn't ask that. Can I say that I found out that he was gay?'

'I wouldn't believe you.'

'Rats.'

'So...'

'Gemma, did Alan ever volunteer to be a sperm donor?' Nate asked, and he watched as she took that on board. Her face changed. To even deeper confusion.

'Yes. Yes, he did. Just before we were married. I wasn't keen on it, but they were advertising round the hospital and he thought it'd be great...'

'To spread his seed a little? I can see that in him. But he only did it the once?'

'He said once was enough.' She was thinking it through. 'But I remember...his mother was so pleased that he'd done it because he'd had mumps really badly as a teenager and she'd been worried that...' Her voice trailed away to a note of discovery. 'Oh.'

'Oh's right. So he'll have donated sperm. He'll have been tested for fertility. In Sydney Central's pathology lab. Who knows what he was told? But we can guess. Maybe that's why he didn't go back again. And if... Maybe if he was told he was infertile but then your sister told him she was carrying his child...'

She was staring in open-mouthed amazement. 'Of course. That was why...'

'Why he forgot about your salary? Why he dumped you

faster than he could look at you and moved in with Fiona? A beautiful woman like Fiona who was telling the world that she was carrying his child? Wow! He'd married you for money but even to a creep like Alan some things are better than money.'

'So then…' Gemma was still thinking it through. 'Cady wasn't his?'

'No, Gemma, Cady wasn't his. And maybe deep down he knew it. Maybe that's why he could treat Cady so dreadfully.'

'Then who? Who is his father?'

'I don't know. Does it matter?'

She thought about that for a whole two seconds and shook her head. 'Of course not. If it's not Alan. Oh, joy, if it's not Alan…'

Bleakness was disappearing by the moment and a brightness was appearing that he'd never seen before. It was as if a weight had been lifted that had been too great to be borne.

'Fiona wanted to hurt me so badly…' she said slowly. 'She would have lied to anyone. Nate, how do you know all this?'

The answer to that was easy. 'I don't.'

'But…'

He placed a finger on her lips. His baby was sleeping peacefully against his chest. The kookaburras were at it again in the gums above their heads, their laughter a glorious background for the crazy conversation happening on the veranda. The morning sun was on their faces, and the world was righting itself. It was as it should be.

Time is to come.

'Gemma, I can't tell you how I know,' Nate said softly. 'If I'm queried then I don't know. Suffice it to say that people have broken a few rules on your behalf. Because they care about you.'

She was still taking it on board. 'Someone...someone from Sydney Central told you that Alan's infertile?'

'No one told me anything.'

'Yeah. Right. And if he'd called your bluff...'

'Then we'd both have done DNA testing, and we both would have been horrified to find that neither of us was the father. But that's not going to happen. You saw Alan's face. He won't come near us again. So until anything happens to the contrary, we assume I'm Cady's father. As you're his mother.'

'But...'

'And as you'll be my wife.'

For a long, long moment neither of them spoke. Words weren't necessary. What was between them was too new, too amazing and too infinitely precious for speech.

Neither did they touch. They sat side by side, staring out at the morning sunshine over the river.

Here was her home.

Gemma's heart felt as if it was close to bursting. She felt like she was close to bursting. The enormity of what she'd just been granted... The lifting of a burden to be replaced by such sweet promise...

Her Nate...

Her love.

'Will you marry me?' he asked at last, and she closed her eyes as if in pain.

'You don't have to. Just because...'

'Just because why?'

'Just because you can.'

He grinned. 'Now, there's a statement. Just because I can means you just said yes.'

'I can see I'm going to have to watch you,' she said, but there was lovely laughter breaking through her voice. 'You twist a girl's words. You lie and you cheat. You write yourself love letters—and you boast about sex!'

'Hey, telling the truth is hardly boasting.'

'Was it great sex?'

He heard the tiny note of pain in her voice and the laughter died. Fiona was rearing her hurtful self again— but this must be the last time she came between them. From this day forth they'd be free. Free to mourn a sister who'd given them two such wonderful children. Free to move on with love.

He took Gemma's face in his hands and cupped her chin. The baby was cradled between them, safely nestled between the two adults who loved her so much.

'No, Gemma, it was not great sex. It was a mistake. An aberration. It was a one-night stand and as soon as I did it I knew it was a mistake. Whereas as soon as I saw you…'

'Yeah, right. You fell in love just like that.' There was a note of derision in her voice—of self-mockery—and he shook his head. He'd have none of it.

'No. I thought you looked brave and warm and caring. I thought you looked like a woman of integrity.' Nate hesitated. 'I didn't know then, of course, that you cheat at Scrabble.'

'Hey…'

He was brooking no interruptions. 'But, of course, you're right. I didn't fall in love with you just like that. It took me two whole weeks to do it. But in those two weeks, Gemma, I've fallen so in love with you that I can never fall out of love. I love you with all my heart, and with all my soul. I never want any woman but you. If you won't marry me then I won't marry anyone.' The seriousness gave way to a smile. 'I'll pine to a shadow of my glorious self.'

'You…pine?'

'I'll definitely pine.' The laughter was back in full now, sparking between them with a warmth that was delicious all by itself. 'So, you see, you have to marry me. It's the only thing a caring doctor can do. To save me from a fate worse than death.'

'Fate worse than death? Pining? Is that a medical condition?'

'The worst. And the only possible prescription is marriage,' he told her. 'The prescription is a wife and two great kids and Uncle Graham and a dog called Rufus and our own Mrs McCurdle…and whoever else happens to come along. Just say yes, my darling heart. Just say yes.'

What was a girl to do?

'Yes,' Gemma whispered.

There was a whoop of triumph and Mia opened her eyes with astonishment. To find she was enveloped in a hug that promised the world.

'Shall we go tell Cady he has a new daddy?' Nate demanded, and Gemma shook her head.

'Not until his daddy's been kissed,' she told him. 'The cure for pining has to start right now.'

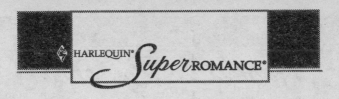

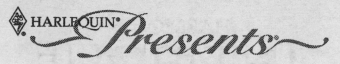

HARLEQUIN *Presents*

The world's bestselling romance series...
The series that brings you your favorite authors,
month after month:

Helen Bianchin...Emma Darcy
Lynne Graham...Penny Jordan
Miranda Lee...Sandra Marton
Anne Mather...Carole Mortimer
Susan Napier...Michelle Reid

and many more uniquely talented authors!

Wealthy, powerful, gorgeous men...
Women who have feelings just like your own...
The stories you love, set in exotic, glamorous locations...

Seduction and passion guaranteed!

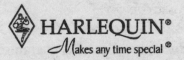